The Unspeakable Perk

Samuel Hopkins Adams

1st WORLD
LIBRARY
Literary Society

The Unspeakable Perk

Samuel Hopkins Adams

© 1st World Library – Literary Society, 2004
PO Box 2211
Fairfield, IA 52556
www.1stworldlibrary.org
First Edition

LCCN: 2004195353

Softcover ISBN: 1-4218-0187-6
Hardcover ISBN: 1-4218-0087-X
eBook ISBN: 1-4218-0287-2

Purchase *"The Unspeakable Perk"*
as a traditional bound book at:
www.1stWorldLibrary.org/purchase.asp?ISBN=1-4218-0187-6

*The **Unspeakable Perk***
contributed by Tim, Ed & Rodney
in support of
1st World Library Literary Society

CONTENTS

I

MR. BEETLE MAN

The man sat in a niche of the mountain, busily hating the Caribbean Sea. It was quite a contract that he had undertaken, for there was a large expanse of Caribbean Sea in sight to hate; very blue, and still, and indifferent to human emotions. However, the young man was a good steadfast hater, and he came there every day to sit in the shade of the overhanging boulder, where there was a little trickle of cool air down the slope and a little trickle of cool water from a crevice beneath the rock, to despise that placid, unimpressionable ocean and all its works and to wish that it would dry up forthwith, so that he might walk back to the blessed United States of America. In good plain American, the young man was pretty homesick.

Two-man's-lengths up the mountain, on the crest of the sturdy hater's rock, the girl sat, loving the Caribbean Sea. Hers, also, was a large contract, and she was much newer to it than was the man to his, for she had only just discovered this vantage-ground by turning accidentally into a side trail - quite a private little side trail made by her unsuspected neighbor below - whence one emerges from a sea of verdure into full view of the sea of azure. For the time, she was content to rest there in the flow of the breeze and feast her eyes on that broad, unending blue which blessedly separated her from the United States of America and certain perplexities and complications comprised therein. Presently she would resume the trail and return to the city of Caracuna, somewhere behind her. That is, she would if she could find it, which was by no means certain. Not that she greatly cared. If she were really lost, they'd come out and get her. Meantime, all she wished was to rest mind and body in the contemplation of that restful plain of cool sapphire, four thousand feet below.

But there was a spirit of mischief abroad upon that mountain slope. It embodied itself in a puff of wind that stirred gratefully the curls above the girl's brow. Also, it fanned the neck of the watcher below and cunningly moved his hat from his side; not more than a few feet, indeed, but still far enough to transfer it from the shade into the glaring sun and into the view of the girl above. The owner made no move. If the wind wanted to blow his new panama into some lower treetop, compelling him to throw stones, perhaps to its permanent damage, in order to dislodge it, why, that was just one more cause of offense to pin to his indictment of irritation against the great island republic of Caracuna. Such is the temper one gets into after a year in the tropics.

Like as peas are panama hats to the eyes of the inexpert; far more like than men who live under them. For the girl, it was a direct inference that this was a hat which she knew intimately; which, indeed, she had rather maliciously eluded, riot half an hour before. Therefore, she addressed it familiarly: "Boo!"

The result of this simple monosyllable exceeded her

fondest expectations. There was a sharp exclamation of surprise, followed by a cry that might have meant dismay or wrath or both, as something metallic tinkled and slid, presently coming to a stop beside the hat, where it revealed itself as a pair of enormous, aluminum-mounted brown-green spectacles. After it, on all fours, scrambled the owner.

Shock number one: It wasn't the man at all! Instead of the black-haired, flanneled, slender Adonis whom the trouble-maker confidently assumed to have been under that hat, she beheld a brownish-clad, stocky figure with a very blond head.

Shock number two: The figure was groping lamentably and blindly in the undergrowth, and when, for an instant, the face was turned half toward her, she saw that the eyes were squinted tight-closed, with a painful extreme of muscular tension about them.

Presently one of the ranging hands encountered the spectacles, and settled upon them. With careful touches, it felt them all over. A mild grunt, presumably of satisfaction, made itself heard, and the figure got to its feet. But before the face turned again, the girl had stepped back, out of range.

Silence, above and below; a silence the long persistence of which came near to constituting shock number three. What sort of hermit had she intruded upon? Into what manner of remote Brahministic contemplation had she injected that impertinent "Boo!"? Who, what, how, why -

"Say it again." The request came from under the rock. Evidently the spectacled owner had resumed his original situation.

"Say WHAT again?" she inquired.

"Anything," returned the voice, with child-like content.

"Oh, I - I hope you didn't break your glasses."

"No; you didn't."

On consideration, she decided to ignore this prompt countering of the pronoun.

"I thought you were some one else," she observed.

"Well, so I am, am I not?"

"So you are what?"

"Some one else than you thought."

"Why, yes, I suppose - But I meant some one else besides yourself."

"I only wish I were."

"Why?" she asked, intrigued by the fervid inflection of the wish.

"Because then I'd be somewhere else than in this infernal hell-hole of a black-and-tan nursery of revolution, fever, and trouble!"

"I think it one of the loveliest spots I've ever seen," said she loftily.

"How long have you been here?"

"On this rock? Perhaps five minutes."

"Not on the rock. In Caracuna?"

"Quite a long time. Nearly a fortnight."

The commentary on this was so indefinite that she was moved to inquire: -

"Is that a local dialect you're speaking?"

"No; that was a grunt."

"I don't think it was a very polite grunt, even as grunts go."

"Perhaps not. I'm afraid I'm out of the habit."

"Of grunting? You seem expert enough to satisfy -"

"No; of being polite. I'll apologize if - if you'll only go on talking."

She laughed aloud.

"Or laughing," he amended promptly. "Do it again."

"One can't laugh to order!" she protested; "or even talk to order. But why do you stay 'way out here in the mountains if you're so eager to hear the human voice?"

"The human voice be - choked! It's YOUR human voice I want to hear - your kind of human voice, I mean." "I don't know that my kind of human voice is particularly different from plenty of other human voices," she observed, with an effect of fine impartial judgment.

"It's widely different from the kind that afflicts the suffering ear in this part of the world. Fourteen months ago I heard the last American girl speak the last American-girl language that's come within reach of me. Oh, no, - there WAS one, since, but she rasped like a rheumatic phonograph and had brick-colored freckles. Have you got brick-colored freckles?"

"Stand up and see."

"No, SIR! - that is, ma'am. Too much risk."

"Risk! Of what?"

"Freckles. I don't like freckles. Not on YOUR voice, anyway."

"On my VOICE? Are you -"

"Of course I am - a little. Any one is who stays down here more than a year. But that about the voice and the freckles was sane enough. What I'm trying to say - and you might know it without a diagram - is that, from your voice, you ought to be all that a man dreams of when - well, when he hasn't seen a real American girl for an eternity. Now I can sit here and dream of you as the loveliest princess that ever came and went and left a memory of gold and blue in the heart of -"

"I'm not gold and blue!"

"Of course you're not. But your speech is. I'll be wise,

and content myself with that. One look might pull down, In irrevocable ruin, all the lovely fabric of my dream. By the way, are you a Cookie?"

"A WHAT?"

"Cookie. Tourist. No, of course you're not. No tour would be imbecile enough to touch here. The question is: How did you get here?"

"Ah, that's my secret."

"Or, rather, are you here at all? Perhaps you're just a figment of the overstrained ear. And if I undertook to look, there wouldn't be anything there at all."

"Of course, if you don't believe in me, I'll fly away on a sunbeam."

"Oh, please! Don't say that! I'm doing my best."

So panic-stricken was the appeal that she laughed again, in spite of herself.

"Ah, that's better! Now, come, be honest with me. You're not pretty, are you?"

"Me? I'm as lovely as the dawn."

"So far, so good. And have you got long golden - that is to say, silken hair that floats almost to your knees?"

"Certainly," she replied, with spirit.

"Is it plentiful enough so that you could spare a little?"

"Are you asking me for a lock of my hair?" she queried, on a note of mirth. "For a stranger, you go fast."

"No; oh, no!" he protested. "Nothing so familiar. I'm offering you a bribe for conversation at the price of, say, five hairs, if you can sacrifice so many."

"It sounds delightfully like voodoo," she observed. "What must I do with them?"

"First, catch your hair. Well up toward the head, please. Now pull it out. One, two, three - yank!"

"Ouch!" said the voice above.

"Do it again. Now have you got two?"

"Yes."

"Knot them together."

There was a period of silence.

"It's very difficult," complained the girl.

"Because you're doing it in silence. There must be sprightly conversation or the charm won't work. Talk!"

"What about?"

"Tell me who you thought I was when you said, 'Boo!' at me."

"A goose."

"A - a GOOSE! Why - what -"

"Doesn't one proverbially say 'Boo!' to a goose?" she remarked demurely.

"If one has the courage. Now, I haven't. I'm shy."

"Shy! You?" Again the delicious trill of her mirth rang in his ears. "I should imagine that to be the least of your troubles."

"No! Truly." There was real and anxious earnestness in his assurance. "It's because I don't see you. If I were face to face with you, I'd stammer and get red and make a regular imbecile of myself. Another reason why I stick down here and decline to yield to temptation."

"O wise young man! ARE you young? Ouch!"

"Reasonably. Was that the last hair?"

"Positively! I'm scalped. You're a red Indian."

"Tie it on. Now, fasten a hairpin on the end and let it down. All right. I've got it. Wait!" The fragile line of communication twitched for a moment. "Haul, now. Gently!"

Up came the thread, and, as its burden rose over the face of the rock, the girl gave a little cry of delight: -

"How exquisite! Orchids, aren't they?"

"Yes, the golden-brown bee orchid. Just your coloring."

"So it is. How do you know?" she asked, startled.

"From the hair. And your eyes have gold flashes in the brown when the sun touches them."

"Your wits are YOUR eyes. But where do you get such orchids?"

"From my little private garden underneath the rock."

"Life will be a dull and dreary round unless I see that garden."

"No! I say! Wait! Really, now, Miss - er -" There was panic in the protest.

"Oh, don't be afraid. I'm only playing with your fears. One look at you as you chased your absurd spectacles was enough to satisfy my curiosity. Go in peace, startled fawn that you are."

"Go nothing! I'm not going. Neither are you, I hope, until you've told me lots more about yourself."

"All that for a spray of orchids?"

"But they are quite rare ones."

"And very lovely."

The girl mused, and a sudden impulse seized her to take the unseen acquaintance at his word and free her mind as she had not been able to do to any living soul for long weeks. She pondered over it.

"You aren't getting ready to go?" he cried, alarmed at

her long silence.

"No; I'm thinking."

"Please think aloud."

"I was thinking - suppose I did."

There was so much of weighty consideration in her accents that the other fear again beset him.

"Did what? Not come down from the rock?" "Be calm. I shouldn't want to face you any more than you want to face me, if I decided to do it."

"Go on," he encouraged. "It sounds most promising."

"More than that. It's fairly thrilling. It's the awful secret of my life that I'm considering laying bare to you, just like a dime novel. Are you discreet?"

"As the eternal rocks. Prescribe any form of oath and I'll take it."

"I'm feeling just irresponsible enough to venture. Now, if I knew you, of course I couldn't. But as I shall never set eyes on you again - I never shall, shall I?"

"Not unless you creep up on me unawares."

"Then I'll unburden my overweighted heart, and you can be my augur and advise me with supernatural wisdom. Are you up to that?"

"Try me."

"I will. But, remember: this means truly that we are never to meet. And if you ever do meet me and recognize my voice, you must go away at once."

"Agreed," he said cheerfully, just a bit too cheerfully to be flattering.

"Very well, then. I'm a runaway."

"From where?"

"Home."

"Naturally. Where's home?"

"Utica, New York," she specified.

"U.S.A.," he concluded, with a sigh. "What did you run away from?"

"Trouble."

"Does any one ever run away from anything else?" he inquired philosophically. "What particular brand?"

"Three men," she said dolorously. "All after poor little me. They all thought I ought to marry them, and everybody else seemed to think so, too -"

"Go slow! Did you say Utica or Utah?"

"Everybody thought I ought to marry one or the other of 'em, I mean. If I could have married them all, now, it might have been easier, for I like them ever so much. But how could I make up my mind? So I just seized papa around the neck and ran away with him down here."

"Why here, of all places on earth?"

"Oh, he's interested in some mines and concessions and things. It's very beautiful, but I almost wish I'd stayed at home and married Bobby."

"Which is Bobby?"

"He's one of the home boys. We've grown up together, and I'm so fond of him. Only it's more the brother-and-sister sort of thing, if he'd let it be."

"Check off No. 1. What's No. 2?"

"Lots older. Mr. Thomas Murray Smith is an unspoiled millionaire. If he weren't so serious and quite so dangerously near forty - well, I don't know."

"Have you kept No. 3 for the last because he's the best?"

"No-o-o-o. Because he's the nearest. He followed me down. You can see his name in all its luster on the Hotel Kast register, when you get back to the city - Preston Fairfax Fitzhugh Carroll, at your service."

"Sounds Southern," commented the man below.

"Southern! He's more Southern than the South Pole. His ancestors fought all the wars and owned all the negroes - he calls them 'niggers' - and married into all the first families of Virginia, and all that sort of thing. He must quite hate himself, poor Fitz, for falling in love with a little Yankee like me. In fact, that's why I made him do it."

"And now you wish he hadn't?"

"Oh - well - I don't know. He's awfully good-looking and gallant and devoted and all that. Only he's such a prickly sort of person. I'd have to spend the rest of my life keeping him and his pride out of trouble. And I've no taste for diplomacy. Why, only last week he declined to dine with the President of the Republic because some one said that his excellency had a touch of the tar brush."

"He'd better get out of this country before that gets back to headquarters."

"If he thought there was danger, he'd stay forever. I don't suppose Fitz is afraid of anything on earth. Except perhaps of me," she added after-thoughtfully.

"Young woman, you're a shameless flirt!" accused the invisible one in stern tones.

"If I am, it isn't going to hurt you. Besides, I'm not. And, anyway, who are you to judge me? You're not here as a judge; you're an augur. Now, go on and aug."

"Aug?" repeated the other hesitantly.

"Certainly. Do an augury. Tell me which."

"Oh! As for that, it's easy. None."

"Why not?"

"Because I much prefer to think of you, when you are

gone, as unmarried. It's more in character with your voice."

"Well, of all the selfish pigs! Condemned to be an old maid, in order not to spoil an ideal! Perhaps you'd like to enter the lists yourself," she taunted.

"Good Heavens, no!" he cried in the most unflattering alarm. "It isn't in my line - I mean I haven't time for that sort of thing. I'm a very busy man."

"You look it! Or you did look it, scrambling about like a doodle bug after your absurd spectacles."

"There is no such insect as a doodle bug."

"Isn't there? How do you know? Are you personally acquainted with all the insect families?"

"Certainly. That's my business. I'm a scientist."

"Oh, gracious! And I've appealed to you in a matter of sentiment! I might better have stuck to Fitz. Poor Fitz! I wonder if he's lost."

"Why should he be lost?"

"Because I lost him. Back there on the trail. Purposely. I sent him for water and then - I skipped."

"Oh-h-h! Then HE'S the goose."

"Goose! Preston Fairfax Fitz -"

"Yes, the goose you said 'Boo!' to, you know."

"Of course. You didn't steal his hat, did you?"

"No. It's my own hat. Why did you run away from him?"

"He bored me. When people bore me, I always run away. I'm beginning to feel quite fugitive this very minute."

There was silence below, a silence that piqued the girl.

"Well," she challenged, "haven't you anything to say before the court passes sentence of abandonment to your fate?"

"I'm thinking - frantically. But the thoughts aren't girl thoughts. I mean, they wouldn't interest you. I might tell you about some of my insects," he added hopefully.

"Heaven forbid!"

"They're very interesting."

"No. You're worthless as an augur, and a flat failure as a conversationalist, when thrown on your own resources. So I shall shake the dust from my feet and depart."

"Good-bye!" he said desolately. "And thank you."

"For what?"

"For making music in my desert."

"That's much better," she approved. "But you've paid

your score with the orchids. If you have one or two more pretty speeches like that in stock, I might linger for a while."

"I'm afraid I'm all out of those," he returned. "But," he added desperately, "there's the hexagonal scarab beetle. He's awfully queer and of much older family even than Mr. Fitzwhizzle's. It is the hexagonal scarab's habit when dis -"

"We have an encyclopaedia of our own at home," she interrupted coldly. "I didn't climb this mountain to talk about beetles."

"Well, I'll talk some more about you, if you'll give me a little time to think."

"I think you are very impertinent. I don't wish to talk about myself. Just because I asked your advice in my difficulties, you assume that I'm a little egoist -"

"Oh, please don't - "

"Don't interrupt. I'm very much offended, and I'm glad we are never going to meet. Just as I was beginning to like you, too," she added, with malice. "Good-bye!"

"Good-bye," he answered mournfully.

But his attentive ears failed to discern the sound of departing footsteps. The breeze whispered in the tree-tops. A sulphur-yellow bird, of French extraction, perched in a flowering bush, insistently demanded: "Qu'est-ce qu'il dit? Qu'est-ce qu'il dit?" - What's he say? WHAT'S he say? - over and over again, becoming quite wrathful because neither he nor any one else offered the slightest reply or explanation. The girl sympathized with the bird. If the particular he whose blond top she could barely see by peeping over the rock would only say something, matters would be easier for her. But he didn't. So presently, in a voice of suspiciously saccharine meekness, she said: -

"Please, Mr. Beetle Man, I'm lost."

"No, you're not," he said reassuringly. "You're not a quarter of a mile from the Puerto del Norte Road."

"But I don't know which direction -"

"Perfectly simple. Keep on over the top of the rock; turn left down the slope, right up the dry stream bed to a dead tree; bear right past -"

"That's too many turns, I never could remember more than two."

"Now, listen," he said persuasively. "I can make it quite plain to you if -"

"I don't WISH to listen! I'll never find it."

"I'll toss you up my compass."

"I don't want your compass," she said firmly.

A long patient sigh exhaled from below.

"Do you want me to guide you?"

"No," she retorted, and was instantly panic-stricken, for the monosyllable was of that accent which sets fire to bridges and burns them beyond hope of return.

Slowly she got to her feet. Perhaps she would have dared and gone; perhaps she would have swallowed pride and her negative, and made one more appeal. She turned hesitantly and saw the devil.

It was a small devil on stilts, not more than three or four inches tall, but there was no mistaking his identity. No other living thing could possess such demoniac little red-hot pin points of eyes, or be so bristly and grisly and vicious. The stilts suddenly folded flat, and the devil rushed upon his prey. The girl stepped back; her foot turned and caught, and -

"Of course," the patient voice below was saying, "if you really think that you couldn't find the road, I could draw you a map and send it up by the hair route. But I really think -"

"BLUMP!"

The rock had turned over on his unprotected head and flattened him out forever. Such was his first thought. When he finally collected himself, his eyeglasses, and his senses, he sustained a second shock more violent than the first.

Two paces away, the Voice, duly and most appropriately embodied, sat half-facing him. The Voice's eyes confirmed his worst suspicions, and, dazed though they were at the moment, there were deep lights in them that wholly disordered his mental mechanism. Nor were her first words such as to restore his deranged faculties.

"Oh-h! Aren't you GOGGLESOME!" she cried dizzily.

He raised his hands to the huge brown spectacles.

"Wh - wh - what did you come down for?" he babbled. There was a distinct note of accusation in the query.

"COME down! I fell!"

"Yes, yes; that may be true -"

"MAY be!"

"Of course, it is true. I - I - I see it's true. I'm awfully sorry."

"Sorry? What for?"

"That you came. That you fell, I mean to say. I - I - I don't really know what I mean to say."

"No wonder, poor boy! I landed right on you, didn't I?"

"Did you? Something did. I thought it was the mountain."

"You aren't very complimentary," she pouted. "But there! I dare say I knocked your thoughts all to bits."

"No; not at all. Certainly, I mean. It doesn't matter. See here," he said, with an injured sharpness of inquiry born of his own exasperation at his verbal fumbling, "you said you wouldn't, and here you are. I ask you, is that fair and honorable?"

" Well , if it comes to that , " she countered , " you

promised that you'd never speak to me if you saw me, and here you are telling me that you don't want me around the place at all. It's very rude and inhospitable, I consider."

"I can't help it," he said miserably. "I'm afraid."

"You don't look it. You look disagreeable."

"As long as you stayed where you belonged - Excuse me - I don't mean to be impolite - but I - I - You see - as long as you were just a voice, I could manage all right, but now that you are - er - er - you -" His speech trailed off lamentably into meaningless stutterings.

The girl turned amazed and amused eyes upon him.

"What on earth ails the poor man?" she inquired of all creation.

"I told you. I - I'm shy."

"Not really! I thought it was a joke."

"Qu'est-ce qu'il dit? Qu'est-ce qu'il dit?" demanded the yellow-breasted inquisitor, from his flowery perch.

"What does he say? He says he's shy. Poor poo - er young, helpless thing!" And her laughter put to shame a palm thrush who was giving what he had up to that moment considered a highly creditable musical performance.

"All right!" he retorted warmly. "Laugh if you want to! But after stipulating that we should be strangers, to - to act this way - well, I think it's - it's - forward. That's what I think it is."

"Do you, indeed? Perhaps you think it's pleasant for me, after I've opened my heart to a stranger, to have him forced on me as an acquaintance!"

From the depths of those limpid eyes welled up a little film of vexation.

"O Lord! Don't do that!" he implored. "I didn't mean - I'm a bear - a pig - a - a - a scarab - I'm anything you choose. Only don't do that!"

"I'm not doing anything."

"Of course you're not. That's fine! As for your secrets, I dare say I wouldn't know you again if I saw you."

"Oh, wouldn't you?" she cried in quite another tone.

"Quite likely not. These glasses, you see. They make things look quite queer."

"Or if you heard me?" she challenged.

"Ah, well, that's different. But I forget quite easily - even things like voices."

She leaned forward, her hands in her lap, her eyes upon the goggled face before her.

"Then take them off."

"What? My glasses?"

"Take them off!"

"Wh - wh - why should I?"

"So that you can see me better."

"I don't want to see you better."

"Yes, you do. I'm much more interesting than a scarab."

"But I know about scarabs and I don't know about - about -"

"Girls. So one might suspect. Do you know what I'm doing, Mr. Beetle Man?"

"N-n-no."

"I'm flirting with you. I never flirted with a scientific person before. It's awfully one-sided, difficult, uphill work."

This last was all but drowned out in his flood of panicky instructions, from which she disentangled such phrases as "first to left" - "dry river-bed-hundred-yards" - "dead tree - can't miss it."

"If you send me away now, I'll cry. Really, truly cry, this time."

"No, you won't! I mean I won't! I - I'll do anything! I'll talk! I'll make conversation! How old are you? That's what the Chinese ask. I used to have a Chinese cook, but he lost all my shirt studs, playing fan-tan. Can you play fan-tan? Two can't play, though. They have funny cards in this country, like the Spanish. Have you seen a bullfight yet ? Don't do it. It's dull and brutal. The bull has no more chance than - than -"

"Than an unprotected man with a conscienceless flirt, who falls on his neck and then threatens to submerge him in tears."

"Now you're beginning again!" he wailed. "What did you jump for, anyway?"

"I slipped. An awful, red-eyed, scrambly fiend scared me - a real, live, hairy devilkin on stilts. He ran at me across the rock. Was that one of your pet scarabs, Mr. Beetle Man?"

"That was a tarantula, I suppose, from the description."

"They're deadly, aren't they?"

"Of course not. Unscientific nonsense. I'll go up and chase him off."

"Flying from perils that you know not of to more familiar dangers?" she taunted.

"Well, you see, with the tarantula out of the way, there's no reason why you shouldn't - er -"

"Go, and leave you in peace? What do you think of that for gallantry, Birdie?"

The gay-feathered inquisitor had come quite near.

"Qu'est-ce qu'il dit?" he queried, cocking his curious head.

"He says he doesn't like me one little, wee, teeny bit,

and he wishes I'd go home and stay there. And so I'm going, with my poor little feelings all hurted and ruffled up like anything."

"Nothing of the sort," protested the badgered spectacle-wearer.

"Then why such unseemly haste to make my path clear?"

"I just thought that maybe you'd go back on the top of the rock, where you came from, and - and be a voice again. If you won't go, I will."

He made three jumps of it up the boulder, bearing a stick in his hand. Presently his face, preternaturally solemn and gnomish behind the goggles, protruded over the rim. The girl was sitting with her hands folded in her lap, contemplating the scenery as if she'd never had another interest in her life. Apparently she had forgotten his very existence.

"Ahem!" he began nervously.

"Ahem!" she retorted so promptly that he almost fell off his precarious perch. "Did you ring? Number, please."

"I wish I knew whether you were laughing at me or not," he said ruefully.

"When?"

"All the time."

"I am. Your darkest suspicions are correct. Did you

abolish my devilkin?"

"I drove him back into his trapdoor home and put a rock over it."

"Why didn't you destroy him?"

"Because I've appointed him guardian of the rock, with strict instructions to bite any one that ever comes there after this except you."

"Bravo! You're progressing. As soon as you're free from the blight of my regard, you become quite human. But I'll never come again."

"No, I suppose not," he said dismally. "I shan't hear you again, unless, perhaps, the echoes have kept your voice to play with."

"Oh, oh! Is this the language of science? You know I almost think I should like to come - if I could. But I can't."

"Why not?"

"Because we leave to-morrow."

" Not across to the southern coast ? It isn't safe. Fever -"

"No; by Puerto del Norte."

"There's no boat."

"Yes, there is. You can just see her funnel over that white slope. It's our yacht."

"And you think you are going in her to-morrow?"

"Think? I know it."

"No," he contradicted.

"Yes," she asserted, quite as concisely.

"No," he repeated. "You're mistaken."

"Don't be absurd. Why?" "Look out there, over that tree to the horizon."

"I'm looking."

"Do you see anything?"

"Yes; a sort of little smudge."

"That's why."

"It's a very shadowy sort of why."

"There's substance enough under it."

"A riddle? I'll give it up."

"No; a bet. I'll bet you the treasures of my mountain-side. Orchids of gold and white and purple and pink, butterflies that dart on wings of fire opal -"

"Beetles, to know which is to love them, and love but them forever," she laughed. "And my side of the wager - what is that to be?"

"That you will come to the rock day after to-morrow at

this hour and stand on the top and be a voice again and talk to me."

"Done! Send your treasures to the pier, for you'll surely lose. And now take me to the road."

It was a single-file trail, and he walked in advance, silent as an Indian. As they emerged from a thicket into the highway, above the red-tiled city in its setting of emerald fields strung on the silver thread of the Santa Clara River, she turned and gave him her hand.

"Be at your rock to-morrow, and when you see the yacht steam out, you'll know I'll be saying good-bye, and thank you for your mountain treasures. Send them to Miss Brewster, care of the yacht Polly. She's named after me. Is there anything the matter with my shoes?" she broke off to inquire solicitously.

"Er - what? No." He lifted his eyes, startled, and looked out across the quaint old city.

"Then is there anything the matter with my face?"

"Yes."

"Yes? Well, what?"

"It's going to be hard to forget," complained he of the goggles.

"Then look away before it's too late," she cried merrily; but her color deepened a little. "Good-bye, O friend of the lowly scarab!"

At the dip of the road down into the bridged arroyo,

she turned, and was surprised - or at least she told herself so - to find him still looking after her.

II

AT THE KAST

One dines at the Gran Hotel Kast after the fashion of a champignon sous cloche. The top of the cloche is of fluted glass, with a wide aperture between it and the sides, to admit the rain in the wet season and the flies in the dry. Three balconies run up from the dining-room well to this roof, and upon these, as near to the railings as they choose, the rather conglomerate patronage of the place sleeps, takes baths, dresses, gossips, makes love, quarrels, and exchanges prophecies as to next Sunday's bullfight, while the diners below strive to select from the bill of fare special morsels upon which they will stake their internal peace for the day. No cabaret can hold a candle to it for variety of interest. When the sudden torrential storms sweep down the mountains at meal times, the little human champignons, beneath their insufficient cloche, rush about wildly seeking spots where the drippage will not wash their food away. Commercial travelers of the tropics have a saying: "There are worse hotels in the world than the Kast - but why take the trouble?" And, year upon year, they return there for reasons connected with the other hostelries of Caracuna, which I forbear to specify.

To Miss Polly Brewster , the Kast was a place of

romance. Five miles away, as the buzzard flies, she could have dined well, even elegantly, on the Brewster yacht. Would she have done it? Not for worlds! Miss Brewster was entranced by the courtly manners of her waiter, who had lost one ear and no small part of the countenance adjacent thereto, only too obviously through the agency of some edged instrument not wielded in the arts of peace. She was further delightedly intrigued by the abrupt appearance of a romantic-hued gentleman, who thrust out over the void from the second balcony an anguished face, one side of which was profusely lathered, and addressed to all the hierarchy of heaven above, and the peoples of the earth beneath, a passionate protest upon the subject of a cherished and vanished shaving brush; what time, below, the head waiter was hastily removing from sight, though not from memory, a soup tureen whose agitated surface bore a creamy froth not of a lacteal origin. One may not with impunity balance personal implements upon the too tremulous rails of the ancient Kast.

With an appreciative and glowing eye, Miss Brewster read from her mimeographed bill of fare such legends as "ropa con carne," "bacalao seco," "enchiladas," and meantime devoured chechenaca, which, had it been translated into its just and simple English of "hash," she would not have given to her cat.

Nor did her visual and prandial preoccupations inhibit her from a lively interest in the surrounding Babel of speech in mingled Spanish, Dutch, German, English, Italian, and French, all at the highest pitch, for a few rods away the cathedral bells were saluting Heaven with all the clangor and din of the other place, and only the strident of voice gained any heed in that contest.

Even after the bells paused, the habit of effort kept the voices up. Miss Brewster, dining with her father a few hours after her return from the mountain, absolved her conscience from any intent of eavesdropping in overhearing the talk of the table to the right of her. The remark that first fixed her attention was in English, of the super-British patois.

"Can't tell wot the blighter might look like behind those bloomin' brown glasses."

"But he's not bothersome to any one," suggested a second speaker, in a slightly foreign accent. "He regards his own affairs."

"Right you are, bo!" approved a tall, deeply browned man of thirty, all sinewy angles, who, from the shoulders up, suggested nothing so much as a club with a gnarled knob on the end of it, a tough, reliable, hardwood club, capable of dealing a stiff blow in an honest cause. "If he deals in conversation, he must SELL it. I don't notice him giving any of it away."

"He gave some to Kast the last time he dined here," observed a languid and rather elegant elderly man, who occupied the fourth side of the table. "Mine host didn't like it."

"I should suppose Senior Kast would be hardened," remarked the young Caracunan who had defended the absent.

"Our eyeglassed friend scored for once, though. They had just served him the usual table-d'hote salad - you know, two leaves of lettuce with a caterpillar on one. Kast happened to be passing. Our friend beckoned him over. 'A little less of the fauna and more of the flora, Senior Kast,' said he in that gritty, scientific voice of his. I really thought Kast was going to forget his Swiss blood, and chase a whole peso of custom right out of the place."

"If you ask me, I think the blighter is barmy," asserted the Briton.

"Well, I'll ask you," proffered the elegant one kindly. "Why do you consider him 'barmy,' as you put it?"

"When I first saw him here and heard him speak to the waiter, I knew him for an American Johnny at once, and I went, directly I'd finished my soup, and sat down at his table. The friendly touch, y' know. 'I say,' I said to him, 'I don't know you, but I heard you speak, and I knew at once you were one of these Americans - tell you at once by the beastly queer accent, you know. You are an American, ay - wot?' Wot d' you suppose the blighter said? He said, 'No, I'm an ichthyo' - somethin' or other -"

"Ichthyosaurus, perhaps," supplied the Caracunuan, smiling.

"That's it, whatever it may be. 'I'm an ichthyosaurus,' he says. 'It's a very old family, but most of the buttons are off. Were you ever bitten by one in the fossil state? Very exhilaratin', but poisonous,' he says. 'So don't let me keep you any longer from your dinner.' Of course, I saw then that he was a wrong un, so I cut him dead, and walked away."

"Served him right," declared the elderly American, with a solemn twinkle directed at the tall brown man, who, having opened his mouth, now thought better of it, and closed it again, with a grin.

"But he is very kind," said the native. "When my brother fell and broke his arm on the mountain, this gentleman found him, took care of him, and brought him in on muleback."

"Lives up there somewhere, doesn't he, Mr. Raimonda?" asked the big man.

"In the quinta of a deserted plantation," replied the Caracunan.

"Wot's he do?" asked the Englishman.

"Ah, THAT one does not know, unless Senor Sherwen can tell us."

"Not I," said the elderly man. "Some sort of scientific investigation, according to the guess of the men at the club."

"You never can tell down here," observed the Englishman darkly. "Might be a blind, you know. Calls himself Perkins. Dare say it isn't his name at all."

"Daughter," said Mr. Thatcher Brewster at this juncture, in a patient and plaintive voice, "for the fifth and last time, I implore you to pass me the butter, or that which purports to be butter, in the dish at your elbow."

"Oh, poor dad! Forgive me! But I was overhearing some news of an - an acquaintance."

"Do you know any of the gentlemen upon whose conversation you are eavesdropping?"

In financial circles, Mr. Brewster was credited with the possession of a cold blue eye and a denatured voice of interrogation, but he seldom succeeded in keeping a twinkle out of the one and a chuckle out of the other when conversing with his daughter.

"Not yet," observed that damsel calmly.

"Meaning, I suppose I am to understand -"

"Precisely. Haven't you noticed them looking this way? Presently they'll be employing all their strategy to meet me. They'll employ it on you."

Mr. Brewster surveyed the group dubiously.

"In a country such as this, one can't be too - too cau -"

"Too particular, as you were saying," cut in his daughter cheerfully. "Men are scarce - except Fitzhugh, who is rather less scarce than I wish he were lately. You know," she added, with a covert glance at the adjoining table, "I wouldn't be surprised if you found yourself an extremely popular papa immediately after dinner. It might even go so far as cigars. Do you suppose that lovely young Caracunan is a bullfighter?"

"No; I believe he's a coffee exporter. Less romantic, but more respectable. Quite one of the gilded youth of Caracuna. His name is Raimonda. Fitzhugh knows him. By the way, where on earth is Fitzhugh?"

"Trying to fit a kind and gentlemanly expression over a

swollen sense of injury, for a guess," replied the girl carelessly. "I left him in sweet and lone communion with nature three hours ago."

"Polly, I wish -"

"Oh, dad, dear, don't! You'll get your wish, I suppose, and Fitz, too. Only I don't want to be hurried. Here he is, now. Look at that smile! A sculptor couldn't have done any better. Now, as soon as he comes, I'm going to be quite nice and kind."

But Mr. Fairfax Preston Fitzhugh Carroll did not come direct to the Brewster table. Instead, he stopped to greet the elderly man in the near-by group, and presently drew up a chair. At first, their conversation was low-toned, but presently the young native added his more vivacious accents.

"Who can tell?" the Brewsters heard him say, and marked the fatalistic gesture of the upturned hands. "They disappear. One does not ask questions too much."

"Not here," confirmed the big man. "Always room for a few more in the undersea jails, eh?"

"Always. But I think it was not that with Basurdo. I think it was underground, not undersea." He brushed his neck with his finger tips.

"Is it dangerous for foreigners?" asked Carroll quickly.

"For every one," answered Sherwen; adding significantly: "But the Caracunan Government does not approve of loose fostering of rumors."

Carroll rose and came over to the Brewsters.

"May I bring Mr. Graydon Sherwen over and present him?" he asked. "I can vouch for him, having known his family at home, and -"

"Oh, bring them all, Fitzhugh," commanded the girl.

The exponent of Southern aristocracy looked uncomfortable.

" As to the others ," he said, "Mr. Raimonda is a native -"

"With the manners of a prince. I've quite fallen in love with him already," she said wickedly.

"Of course, if you wish it. But the other American is an ex-professional baseball player, named Cluff."

"What? 'Clipper' Cluff? I knew I'd seen him before!" cried Miss Polly. "He got his start in the New York State League. Why, we're quite old friends, by sight."

"As for Galpy, he's an underbred little cockney bounder."

"With the most naive line of conversation I've ever listened to. I want all of them."

"Let me bring Sherwen first," pleaded the suitor, and was presently introducing that gentleman. "Mr. Sherwen is in charge here of the American Legation," he explained.

" How does one salute a real live minister?" queried

Miss Brewster.

"Don't mistake me for anything so important," said Sherwen. "We're not keeping a minister in stock at present. My job is being a superior kind of janitor until diplomatic relations are resumed."

"Goodness! It sounds like war," said Miss Brewster hopefully. "Is there anything as exciting as that going on?"

"Oh, no. Just a temporary cessation of civilities between the two nations. If it weren't indiscreet - "

"Oh, do be indiscreet!" implored the girl, with clasped hands. "I admire indiscretion in others, and cultivate it in myself."

Mr. Carroll looked pained, as the other laughed and said: -

"Well, it would certainly be most undiplomatic for me to hint that the great and friendly nation of Hochwald, which wields more influence and has a larger market here than any other European power, has become a little jealous of the growing American trade. But the fact remains that the Hochwald minister and his secretary, Von Plaanden, who is a very able citizen when sober, - and is, of course, almost always sober, - have not exerted themselves painfully to compose the little misunderstanding between President Fortuno and us. The Dutch diplomats, who are not as diplomatic in speech as I am, would tell you, if there were any of them left here to tell anything, that Von Plaanden's intrigues brought on the present break with them. So there you have a brief, but reliable 'History of Our

Times in the Island Republic of Caracuna.'"

"Highly informative and improving to the untutored mind," Miss Brewster complimented him. "I like seeing the wires of empire pulled. More, please."

"Perhaps you won't like the next so well," observed Carroll grimly. "There is bubonic plague here."

"Oh - ah!" protested Sherwen gently. "The suspicion of plague. Quite a different matter."

"Which usually turns out to be the same, doesn't it?" inquired Mr. Brewster.

"Perhaps. People disappear, and one is not encouraged to ask about them. But then people disappear for many causes in Caracuna. Politics here are somewhat - well - Philadelphian in method. But - there is smoke rising from behind Capo Blanco."

"What is there?" inquired the girl.

"The lazaretto. Still, it might be yellow fever, or only smallpox. The Government is not generous with information. To have plague discovered now would be very disturbing to the worthy plans of the Hochwald Legation. For trade purposes, they would very much dislike to have the port closed for a considerable time by quarantine. The Dutch difficulty they can arrange when they will. But quarantine would bring in the United States, and that is quite another matter. Well, we'll see, when Dr. Pruyn gets here."

"Who is he?" asked Carroll.

"Special-duty man of the United States Public Health Service. The best man on tropical diseases and quarantine that the service has ever had."

"That isn't Luther Pruyn, is it?" inquired Mr. Brewster.

"The same. Do you know him?"

"Yes."

"More than I do, except by reputation."

"He was in my class at college, but I haven't seen him since. I'd be glad to see him again. A queer, dry fellow, but character and grit to his backbone." "I'd supposed he was younger," said Sherwen. "Anyway, he's comparatively new to the service. His rise is the more remarkable. At present, he's not only our quarantine representative, with full powers, but unofficially he acts, while on his roving commission, for the British, the Dutch, the French, and half the South American republics. I suppose he's really the most important figure in the Caracuna crisis - and he hasn't even got here yet. Perhaps our Hochwaldian friends have captured him on the quiet. It would pay 'em, for if there is plague here, he'll certainly trail it down."

"Oh, I'm tired of plague," announced Miss Polly. "Bring the others here and let's all go over to the plaza, where it's cool."

To their open and obvious delight, exhibited jauntily by the Englishman, with awkward and admiring respectfulness by the ball-player, and with graceful ease by the handsome Caracunan, the rest were invited to join the party.

"Don't let them scare you about plague, Miss Brewster," said Cluff, as they found their chairs. "Foreigners don't get it much."

"Oh, I'm not afraid! But, anyway, we shouldn't have time to catch even a cold. We leave to-morrow."

The men exchanged glances.

"How?" inquired Sherwen and Raimonda in a breath.

"In the yacht, from Puerto del Norte."

"Not if it were a British battleship," said Galpy. "Port's closed."

"What? Quarantine already?" said Carroll.

"Quarantine be blowed! It's the Dutch."

"I thought you knew," said Sherwen. "All the town is ringing with the news. It just came in to-night. Holland has declared a blockade until Caracuna apologizes for the interference with its cable."

"And nothing can pass?" asked Mr. Brewster.

"Nothing but an aeroplane or a submarine."

There was a silence. Miss Polly Brewster broke it with a curious question: -

"What day is day after to-morrow?"

Several voices had answered her, but she paid little heed, for there had slipped over her shoulder a brown thin hand holding a cunningly woven closed basket of reedwork. A soft voice murmured something in Spanish.

"What does he say?" asked the girl "For me?"

"He thinks it must be for you," translated Raimonda, "from the description."

"What description?"

"He was told to go to the hotel and deliver it to the most beautiful lady. There could hardly be any mistaking such specific instructions even by an ignorant mountain peon," he added, smiling.

The girl opened the curious receptacle, and breathed a little gasp of delight. Bedded in fern, lay a mass of long sprays aquiver with bells of the purest, most lucent white, each with a great glow of gold at its heart.

"Ah," observed the young Caracunan, "I see that you are persona grata with our worthy President, Miss Brewster."

"President Fortuno?" asked the girl, surprised. "No; not that I'm aware of. Why do you say that?"

"That is his special orchid - almost the official flower. They call it 'the President's orchid.'"

"Has he a monopoly of growing them?" asked Miss Brewster.

"No one can grow them. They die when transplanted

from their native cliffs. But it's only the President's rangers who are daring enough to get them."

"Are they so inaccessible?"

"Yes. They grow nowhere but on the cliff faces, usually in the wildest part of the mountains. Few people except the hunters and mountaineers know where, and it's only the most adventurous of them who go after the flowers."

"Do you suppose this boy got these?" Miss Brewster indicated the shy and dusky messenger.

Raimonda spoke to the boy for a moment.

"No; he didn't collect them. Nor is he one of the President's men. I don't quite understand it."

"Who did gather them?"

"All that he will say is, 'the master.'"

"Oh!" said Miss Brewster, and retired into a thoughtful silence.

"They're very beautiful, aren't they?" continued the Caracunan. "And they carry a pretty sentiment."

"Tell me," commanded the girl, emerging from her reverie.

"The mountaineers say that their fragrance casts a spell which carries the thought back to the giver."

"Is that the language of science?" she queried absently,

with a thought far away.

"But no, senorita, assuredly not," said the young Caracufian. "It is the language - permit that I say it better in French - c'est le langage d'amour."

III

THE BETTER PART OF VALOR

Night fell with the iron clangor of bells, and day broke to the accompaniment of further insensate jangling, for Caracuna City has the noisiest cathedral in the world; and still the graceful gray yacht Polly lay in the harbor at Puerto del Norte, hemmed in by a thin film of smoke along the horizon where the Dutch warship promenaded.

In one of the side caverns off the main dining-room of the Hotel Kast, the yacht's owner, breakfasting with the yacht's tutelary goddess and the goddess's determined pursuer, discussed the blockade. Though Miss Polly Brewster kept up her end of the conversation, her thoughts were far upon a breeze-swept mountain-side. How, she wondered, had that dry and strange hermit of the wilds known the news before the city learned it? With her wonder came annoyance over her lost wager. The beetle man, she judged, would be coolly superior about it. So she delivered herself of sundry stinging criticisms regarding the conduct of the Caracunan Administration in having stupidly involved itself in a blockade. She even spoke of going to see the President and apprising him of her views.

"I'd like to tell him how to run this foolish little

island," said she, puckering a quaintly severe brow.

"Now is the appointed time for you to plunge in and change the course of empire," her father suggested to her. "There's an official morning reception at ten o'clock. We're invited."

"Then I shan't go. I wouldn't give the old goose the satisfaction of going to his fiesta."

"Meaning the noble and patriotic President?" said Carroll. "Treason most foul! The cuartels are full of chained prisoners who have said less."

"Father can go with Mr. Sherwen. I shall do some important shopping," announced Miss Brewster. "And I don't want any one along."

Thus apprised of her intentions, Carroll wrapped himself in gloom, and retired to write a letter.

Miss Polly's shopping, being conducted mainly through the medium of the sign language, presently palled upon her sensibilities, and about twelve o'clock she decided upon a drive. Accordingly she stepped into one of the pretty little toy victorias with which the city swarms.

"Para donde?" inquired the driver.

His fare made an expansive gesture, signifying "Anywhere." Being an astute person in his own opinion, the Jehu studied the pretty foreigner's attire with an appraising eye, profoundly estimated that so much style and elegance could be designed for only one function of the day, whirled her swiftly along the two-mile drive of the Calvario Road, and landed her at the President's palace, half an hour after the reception was over. Supposing from the coachman's signs that she was expected to go in and view some public garden, she paid him, walked far enough to be stopped by the apologetic and appreciative guard, and returned to the highway, to find no carriage in sight. Never mind, she reflected; she needed the exercise. Accordingly, she set out to walk.

But the noonday sun of Caracuia has a bite to it. For a time, Miss Brewster followed the car tracks which were her sure guide from the palace to the Kast; briskly enough, at first. But, after three cars had passed her, she began to think longingly of the fourth. When it stopped at her signal, it was well filled. The most promising ingress appeared to be across the blockade of a robust and much-begilded young man, who was occupying the familiar position of an "end-seat hog," and displaying the full glories of the Hochwaldian dress uniform.

Herr von Plaanden was both sleepy and cross, for, having lingered after the reception to have a word and several drinks with the Minister of Foreign Affairs, he had come forth to find neither coach nor automobile in attendance. There had been nothing for it but the plebeian trolley. Accordingly, when he heard a foreign voice of feminine timbre and felt a light pressure against his knee, he only snorted. What he next felt against his knee was the impact of a half-shove, half-blow, brisk enough to slue him around. The intruder passed by to the vacant seat, while the now thoroughly awakened and annoyed Hochwaldian whirled, to find himself looking into a pair of expressionless brown goggles.

With a snort of fury, the diplomat struck backward. The glasses and the solemn face behind them dodged smartly. The next moment, Herr von Plaanden felt his neck encircled by a clasp none the less warm for being not precisely affectionate. He was pinned. Twisting, he worked one arm loose.

"Be careful!" warned the cool voice of Polly Brewster, addressing her defender. "He's trying to draw his sword."

The gogglesome one's grip slid a little lower. The car had now stopped, and the conductor came forward, brandishing what was apparently the wand of authority, designed to be symbolic rather than utile, since at no point was it thicker than a man's finger. From a safe distance on the running-board, he flourished this, whooping the while in a shrill and dissuasive manner. Somewhere down the street was heard a responsive yell, and a small, jerky, olive-green policia pranced into view.

Thereupon a strange thing happened. The rescuing knight relaxed his grip, leaped the back of his seat, dropped off the car, and darted like a hunted hare across a compound, around a wall, and so into the unknown, deserting his lady fair, if not precisely in the hour of greatest need, at least in a situation fraught with untoward possibilities. Indeed, it seemed as if these possibilities might promptly become actualities, for the diplomat turned his stimulated wrath upon the girl, and was addressing her in tones too emphatic to be mistaken when a large angular form interposed itself, landing with a flying leap on the seat between them.

"Move!" the newly arrived one briefly bade Herr von Plaanden.

Herr von Plaanden, feeling the pressure of a shoulder formed upon the generous lines of a gorilla's, and noting the approach of the policia on the other side, was fain to obey.

"Don't you be scared, miss," said Cluff, turning to the girl. "It's all over."

"I'm not frightened," she said, with a catch in her voice.

"Of course you ain't," he agreed reassuringly. "You just sit quiet -"

"But I - I - I'm MAD, clean through."

"You gotta right. You gotta perfect right. Now, if this was New York, I'd spread that gold-laced guy's face -"

"I'm not angry at him. Not particularly, I mean."

"No?" queried her friend in need. "What got your goat, then?"

Miss Brewster shot a quick and scornful glance over her shoulder.

"Oh, HIM" interpreted the athlete. "Well, he made his get-away like a man with some reason for being elsewhere."

"Reason enough. He was afraid."

"Maybe. Being afraid's a queer thing," remarked her escort academically. "Now, me, I'm afraid of a fuzzy caterpillar. But I ain't exactly timid about other things."

"You certainly aren't. And I don't know how to thank you."

"Aw, that's awright, miss. What else could I do? Our departed friend, Professor Goggle-Eye, when he made his jump, landed right in my shirt front. 'Take my place,' he says; 'I've got an engagement.' Well, I was just moving forward, anyway, so it was no trouble at all, I assure you," asserted the doughty Cluff, achieving a truly elegant conclusion.

"Most fortunate for me," said the girl sweetly. "Mr. Perkins scuttled away like one of his own little wretched beetles. When I see him again -"

"Again? Oh, well, if he's a friend of yours, accourse he'd awtuv stood by -"

"He isn't!" she declared, with unnecessary vehemence.

"Don't you be too hard on him, miss," argued her escort. "Seems to me he did a pretty good job for you, and stuck to it until he found some one else to take it up."

"Then why didn't he stand by you?"

"Oh, I don't carry any 'Help-wanted' signs on me. You know, miss, you can't size up a man in this country like he was at home. Now, me, I'd have natcherly hammered that Von Plaanden gink all to heh - heh - hash. But did I do it? I did not. You see, I got a little mining concession out here in the mountains, and if I was to get into any diplomatic mix-up and bring in the police, it'd be bad for my business, besides maybe getting me a couple of tons of bracelets around my pretty little ankles. Like as not your friend, Professor Lamps, has got an equally good reason for keeping the peace."

"Do you mean that this man will make trouble for you over this?"

"Not as things stand. So long as nothing was done - no arrests or anything like that - he'll be glad to forget it, when he sobers up. I'll forget it, too, and maybe, miss, it wouldn't be any harm to anybody if you did a turn at forgetting, yourself."

But neither by the venturesome Miss Polly nor by her athlete servitor was the episode to be so readily dismissed. Late that afternoon, when the Brewster party were sitting about iced fruit drinks amid the dingy and soiled elegance of the Kast's one private parlor, Mr. Sherwen's card arrived, followed shortly by Mr. Sherwen's immaculate self, creaseless except for one furrow of the brow.

"How you are going to get out of here I really don't know," he said.

"Why should we hurry?" inquired Miss Brewster. "I don't find Caracuna so uninteresting."

"Never since I came here has it been so charming," said the legation representative, with a smiling bow. "But, much as your party adds to the landscape, I'm not at all sure that this city is the most healthful spot for you at present."

"You mean the plague?" asked Mr. Brewster.

"Not quite so loud, please. 'Healthful,' as I used it, was, in part, a figure of speech. Something is brewing hereabout."

"Not a revolution?" cried Miss Polly, with eyes alight. "Oh, do brew a revolution for me! I should so adore to see one!"

"Possibly you may, though I hardly think it. Some readjustment of foreign relations, at most. The Dutch blockade is, perhaps, only a beginning. However, it's sufficient to keep you bottled up, though if we could get word to them, I dare say they would let a yacht go out."

"Senator Richland, of the Committee on Foreign Relations, is an old friend of my family," said Carroll, in his measured tones. "A cable -"

"Would probably never get through. This Government wouldn't allow it. There are other possibilities. Perhaps, Mr. Brewster," he continued, with a side glance at the girl, "we might talk it over at length this evening."

"Quite useless, Mr. Sherwen," smiled the magnate. "Polly would have it all out of me before I was an hour older. She may as well get it direct."

"Very well, then. It's this quarantine business. If Dr. Pruyn comes here and declares bubonic plague -"

"But how will he get in?" asked Carroll.

"So far as the blockade goes, the Dutch will help him all they can. But this Government will keep him out, if possible."

"He is not persona grata?" asked Brewster.

"Not with any of the countries that play politics with pestilence. But if he's sent here, he'll get in some way. In fact, Stark, the public-health surgeon at Puerto del Norte, let fall a hint that makes me think he's on his way now. Probably in some cockleshell of a small boat manned by Indian smugglers."

"It sounds almost too adventurous for the scholarly Pruyn whom I recall," observed Mr. Brewster.

"The man who went through the cholera anarchy on the lazar island off Camacho, with one case of medical supplies and two boxes of cartridges, may have been scholarly; he certainly didn't exhibit any distaste for adventure. Well, I wish he'd arrive and get something settled. Only I'd like to have you out of the way first."

"Oh, don't send ME away, Mr. Sherwen," pleaded Miss Polly, with mischief in her eyes. "I'd make the cunningest little office assistant to busy old Dr. Pruyn. And he's a friend of dad's, and we surely ought to wait for him."

"If only I COULD send you! The fact is, Americans won't be very popular if matters turn out as I expect."

"Shall we be confined to our rooms and kept incomunicado, while Dr. Pruyn chases the terrified germ through the streets of Caracuna?" queried the irrepressible Polly.

"You'll probably have to move to the legation, where you will be very welcome, but none too comfortable. The place has been practically closed and sealed for two months."

"I'm sure we should bother you dreadfully," said the girl.

"It would bother me more dreadfully if you got into any trouble. Just this morning there was some kind of an affair on a street car in which some Americans were involved."

Miss Polly's countenance was a design - a very dainty and ornamental design - in insouciance as her father said: -

"Americans? Any one we have met?"

"No news has come to me. I understand one of the diplomatic corps, returning from the President's matinee, spoke to an American woman, and an American man interfered."

"When did this happen?" asked Carroll.

"About noon. Inquiries are going on quietly."

The young man directed a troubled and accusing look from his fine eyes upon Miss Brewster.

"You see, Miss Polly," he said, "no lady should go about unprotected down here."

"Ordinarily it's as safe as any city," said Sherwen. "Just now I can't be so certain."

"I hate being watched over like a child!" pouted Miss Brewster. "And I love sight-seeing alone. The flowers along the Calvario Road were so lovely."

"That's the road to the palace," remarked Carroll, looking at her closely.

"And the butterflies are so marvelous," she continued cheerfully. "Who lives in that salmon-pink pagoda just this side of the curve?"

Trouble sat dark and heavy upon the handsome features of Mr. Preston Fairfax Fitzhugh Carroll, but he was too experienced to put a direct query to his inamorata. What suspicion he had, he cherished until after dinner, when he took it to the club and made it the foundation of certain inquiries.

Thus it happened that at eleven o'clock that evening, he paused before a bench in the plaza, bowered in the bloom of creepers which flowed down from a balcony of the Kast, and occupied by the comfortably sprawled-out form of Mr. Thomas Cluff, who was making a burnt offering to Morpheus.

"Good-evening!" said Mr. Carroll pleasantly.

"Evenin'! How's things?" returned the other.

"Right as can be, thanks to you. On behalf of the Brewster family, I want to express our appreciation of your assistance to Miss Brewster this morning."

"Oh, that was nothing," returned the other.

"But it might have been a great deal. Mr. Brewster will

wish to thank you in person -"

"Aw, forget it!" besought Mr. Thomas Cluff. "That little lady is all right. I'd just as soon eat an ambassador, let alone a gilt-framed secretary, to help her out."

"Miss Brewster," said the other, somewhat more stiffly, "is a wholly admirable young lady, but she is not always well advised in going out unescorted. By the way, you can doubtless confirm the rumor as to the identity of her insulter."

"His name is Von Plaanden. But I don't think he meant to insult any one."

"You will permit me to be the best judge of that."

"Go as far as you like," asserted the big fellow cheerfully. "That fellow Perkins can tell you more about the start of the thing than I can."

"From what I hear, he has no cause to be proud of his part in the matter," said the Southerner, frowning.

"He's sure a prompt little runner," asserted Cluff. "But I've run away in my time, and glad of the chance."

"You will excuse me from sympathizing with your standards."

"Sure, you're excused," returned the athlete, so placidly that Carroll, somewhat at a loss, altered his speech to a more gracious tone.

"At any rate, you stood your ground when you were

needed, which is more than Mr. Perkins did. I should like to have a talk with him."

"That's easy. He was rambling around here not a quarter of an hour ago with young Raimonda. That's them sitting on the bench over by the fountain."

"Will you take me over and present me? I think it is due Mr. Perkins that some one should give him a frank opinion of his actions."

"I'd like to hear that," observed Cluff, who was not without humanistic curiosity. "Come along."

Heaving up his six-feet-one from the seat, he led the way to the two conversing men. Raimonda looked around and greeted the newcomers pleasantly. Cluff waved an explanatory hand between his charge and the bench.

"Make you acquainted with Mr. Perkins," he said, neglecting to mention the name of the first party of the introduction.

Perkins, goggling upward to meet a coldly hostile glance, rose, nodded in some wonder, and said: "How do you do?" Raimonda sent Cluff a glance of interrogation, to which that experimentalist in human antagonisms responded with a borrowed Spanish gesture of pleasurable uncertainty.

"I will not say that I'm glad to meet you, Mr. Perkins," began Carroll weightily, and paused.

If he expected a query, he was doomed to a disappointment. Such of the Perkins features as were not concealed by his extraordinary glasses expressed an immovable calm.

"Doubtless you know to what I refer."

Still those blank brown glasses regarded him in silence.

"Do you or do you not?" demanded Carroll, struggling to keep his temper in the face of this exasperating irresponsiveness.

"Haven't the least idea," replied Perkins equably.

"You were on the tram this morning when Miss Brewster was insulted, weren't you?"

"Yes."

"And ran away?"

"I did."

"What did you run away for?"

"I ran away," the other sweetly informed him, "on important business of my own."

Cluff snickered. The suspicion impinged upon Carroll's mind that this wasn't going to be as simple as he had expected.

"Let that go for the moment. Do you know Miss Brewster's insulter?"

"No."

"Are you telling me the truth?" asked the Southerner sternly.

The begoggled one's chin jerked up. To the trained eye of Cluff, swift to interpret physical indications, it seemed that Perkins's weight had almost imperceptibly shifted its center of gravity.

"Our Southern friend is going to run into something if he doesn't look out," he reflected.

But there was no hint of trouble in Perkins's voice as he replied: -

"I know who he is. I don't know him."

"Was it Von Plaanden?"

"Why do you want to know?"

"Because," returned the other, with convincing coolness, "if it was, I intend to slap his face publicly as soon as I can find him."

"You must do nothing of the sort."

Now, indeed, there was a change in the other's bearing. The words came sharp and crisp.

"I shall do exactly as I said. Perhaps you will explain why you think otherwise."

"Because you must have some sense somewhere about you. Do you realize where you are?"

" I hardly think you can teach me geography , or

anything else, Mr. Perkins."

"Well, good God," said the other sharply, "somebody's got to teach you! What do you suppose would be the result of your slapping Von Plaanden's face?"

"Whatever it may be, I am ready. I will fight him with any weapons, and gladly."

"Oh, yes; gladly! Fun for you, all right. But suppose you think of others a little."

"Afraid of being involved yourself?" smiled Carroll. "I'm sure you could run away successfully from any kind of trouble."

"Others might not be so able to escape."

"Of course I'm wholly wrong, and my training and traditions are absurdly old-fashioned, but I've been brought up to believe that the American who will run from a fight, or who will not stand up at home or abroad for American rights, American womanhood, and the American flag, isn't a man."

"Oh, keep it for the Fourth of July," returned Perkins wearily. "You can't get me into a fight."

"Fight?" Carroll laughed shortly. "If you had the traditions of a gentleman, you would not require any more provocation."

"If I had the traditions of a deranged doodle bug, I'd go around hunting trouble in a country that is full of it for foreigners - even those who behave themselves like sane human beings."

"Meaning, perhaps, that I'm not a sane human being?" inquired the Southerner.

"Do you think you act like it? To satisfy your own petty vanity of courage, you'd involve all of us in difficulties of which you know nothing. We're living over a powder magazine here, and you want to light matches to show what a hero you are. Traditions! Don't you talk to me about traditions! If you can serve your country or a woman better by running away than by fighting, the sensible thing to do is to run away. The best thing you can do is to keep quiet and let Von Plaanden drop. Otherwise, you'll have Miss Brewster the center of -"

"Keep your tongue from that lady's name!" warned Carroll.

"You're giving a good many orders," said the other slowly. "But I'll do almost anything just now to keep you peaceable, and to convince you that you must let Von Plaanden strictly alone."

"Just as surely as I meet him," said the Southerner ominously, "on my word of honor -" "Wait a moment," broke in the other sharply. "Don't commit yourself until you've heard me. Just around the corner from here is a cuartel. It isn't a nice clean jail like ours at home. Fleas are the pleasantest companions in the place. When a man - particularly an obnoxious foreigner - lands there, they are rather more than likely to forget little incidentals like food and water. And if he should happen to be of a nation without diplomatic representation here, as is the case with the United States at present, he might well lie there incomunicado until his hearing, which might be in two days or might not be for a month. Is that correct, Mr. Raimonda?"

"Essentially," confirmed the Caracunan.

"When you are through trying to frighten me -" began Carroll contemptuously.

"Frighten you? I'm not so foolish as to waste time that way. I'm trying to warn you."

"Are you quite done?"

"I am not. On MY honor -" He broke off as Carroll smiled. "Smile if you like, but believe what I'm telling you. Unless you agree to keep your hands and tongue off Von Plaanden I'll lay an information which will land you in the cuartel within an hour."

The smile froze on the Southerner's lips.

"Could he do that?" he asked Raimonda.

"I'm afraid he could. And, really, Mr. Carroll, he's correct in principle. In the present state of political feeling, an assault by an American upon the representative of Hochwald might seriously endanger all of your party."

"That's right," Cluff supported him. "I'm with you in wanting to break that gold-frilled geezer's face up into small sections, but it just won't do."

With an effort, Carroll recovered his self-control.

"Mr. Raimonda," he said courteously, "I give YOU my word that there will be no trouble between Herr Von

Plaanden and myself, of my seeking, until Mr. and Miss Brewster are safely out of the country."

"That's enough," said Cluff heartily. "The rest of us can take care of ourselves."

"Meantime," said Raimonda, "I think the whole matter can be arranged. Von Plaanden shall apologize to Miss Brewster to-morrow. It is not his first outbreak, and always he regrets. My uncle, who is of the Foreign Office, will see to it."

"Then that's settled," remarked Perkins cheerfully.

Carroll turned upon him savagely: -

"To your entire satisfaction, no doubt, now that you've shown yourself an informer as well as -"

"Easy with the rough stuff, Mr. Carroll," advised Cluff, his good-natured face clouding. "We're all a little het up. Let's have a drink, and cool down."

"With you, with pleasure. I shall hope to meet you later, Mr. Perkins," he added significantly.

"Well, I hope not," retorted the other. "My voice is still for peace. Meantime, please assure Miss Brewster for me -"

"I warned you to keep that lady's name from your lips."

"You did. But I don't know by what authority. You're not her father, I suppose. Are you her brother, by any chance?"

As he spoke, Perkins experienced that curious feeling that some invisible person was trying to catch his eye. Now, as he turned directly upon Carroll, his glance, passing over his shoulder, followed a broad ray of light spreading from a second-story leaf-framed balcony of the hotel. There was a stir amid the greenery. The face of the Voice appeared, framed in flowers. Its features lighted up with mirth, and the lips formed the unmistakable monosyllable: "Boo!"

The identification was complete - "Boo to a goose."

"Preston Fairfax Fitzhugh Carroll!" Unwittingly he spoke the name aloud, and, unfortunately, laughed.

To a less sensitive temperament, even, than Carroll's, the provocation would have been extreme. Perkins was recalled to a more serious view of the situation by the choking accents of that gentleman.

"Take off your glasses!"

"What for?"

"Because I'm going to thrash you within an inch of your life!"

"Gentlemen, gentlemen!" cried the young Caracunan. "This is no place for such an affair."

Apparently Perkins held the same belief. Stepping aside, he abruptly sat down on the end of the bench, facing the fountain and not four feet from it. His head drooped a little forward; his hands dropped between his knees; one foot - but Cluff, the athlete, was the only one to note this - edged backward and turned to secure a firm hold on the pavement. Carroll stepped over in front of him and stood nonplused. He half drew his hand back, then let it fall.

"I can't hit a man sitting down," he muttered distressfully.

Perkins's set face relaxed.

"Running true to tradition," he observed, pleasantly enough. "I didn't think you would. See here, Mr. Carroll, I'm sorry that I laughed at your name. In fact, I didn't really laugh at your name at all. It was at something quite different which came into my mind at that moment."

"Your apology is accepted so far," returned the other stiffly. "But that doesn't settle the other account between us, when we meet again. Or do you choose to threaten me with jail for that, also?"

"No. It's easier to keep out of your way."

"Good Lord!" cried the Southerner in disgust. "Are you afraid of everything?"

"Why, no!" Perkins rose, smiling at him with perfect equanimity. "As a matter of fact, if you're interested to know, I wasn't particularly afraid of Von Plaanden, and, if I may say so without offense, I'm not particularly afraid of you."

Carroll studied him intently.

"By Jove, I believe you aren't! I give it up!" he cried desperately. "You're crazy, I reckon - or else I am."

And he took himself off without the formality of a farewell to the others.

Raimonda, with a courteous bow to his companions, followed him.

Wearily the goggled one sank back in his seat. Cluff moved across, planting himself exactly where Carroll had stood.

"Perkins!"

"Eh?" responded the sitter absently.

"What would you do if I should bat you one in the eye?"

"Eh, what?"

"What would you do to me?"

"You, too?" cried the bewildered Perkins. "Why on earth -"

"You'd dive into my knees, wouldn't you, and tip me over backward?"

"Oh, that!" A slow grin overspread the space beneath the glasses. "That was the idea."

"I know the trick. It's a good one - except for the guy that gets it."

"It wouldn't have hurt him. He'd have landed in the fountain."

"So he would. What then?"

"Oh, I'd have held him there till he got cooled off, and then made a run for it. A wet man can't catch a dry man."

"Say, son, YOU'RE a dry one, all right."

"Eh?"

"Wake up! I'm saying you're all right."

"Much obliged."

"You certainly took enough off him to rile a sheep. Why didn't you do it?"

"Do what?"

"Tip him in."

Perkins glanced upward at the balcony where the vines had closed upon a face that smiled.

"Oh," he said mildly, "he's a friend of a friend of mine."

IV

TWO ON A MOUNTAIN-SIDE

ORCHIDS do not, by preference, grow upon a cactus plant. Little though she recked of botany, Miss Brewster was aware of this fundamental truth. Neither do they, without extraneous impulsion, go hurtling through the air along deserted mountain-sides, to find a resting-place far below; another natural-history fact which the young lady appreciated without being obliged to consult the literature of the subject. Therefore, when, from the top of the appointed rock, she observed a carefully composed bunch of mauve Cattleyas describe a parabola and finally join two previous clusters upon the spines of a prickly-pear patch, she divined some energizing force back of the phenomenon. That energizing force she surmised was temper.

"Fie!" said she severely. "Beetle gentlemen should control their little feelings. Naughty, naughty!"

From below rose a fervid and startled exclamation.

"Naughtier, naughtier!" deprecated the visitor. "Are these the cold and measured terms of science?"

"You haven't lived up to your bet," complained the

censured one.

"Indeed I have! I always play fair, and pay fair. Here I am, as per contract."

"Nearly half an hour late."

"Not at all. Four-thirty was the time."

"And now it is three minutes to five."

"Making twenty-seven minutes that I've been sitting here waiting for a welcome."

"Waiting? Oh, Miss Brewster -"

"I'm not Miss Brewster. I'm a voice in the wilderness."

"Then, Voice, you haven't been there more than one minute. A voice isn't a voice until it makes a noise like a voice. Q.E.D."

"There is something in that argument," she admitted. "But why didn't you come up and look for me?"

"Does one look for a sound?"

"Please don't be so logical. It tires my poor little brain. You might at least have called."

"That would have been like holding you up for payment of the bet, wouldn't it? I was waiting for you to speak."

"Not good form in Caracuna. The senor should always speak first."

"You began the other time," he pointed out.

"So I did, but that was under a misapprehension. I hadn't learned the customs of the country then. By the way, is it a local custom for hermits of science to climb breakneck precipices for golden-hearted orchids to send to casual acquaintances?"

"Is that what you are?" he queried in a slightly depressed tone.

"What on earth else could I be?" she returned, amused.

"Of course. But we all like to pretend that our fairy tales are permanent, don't we?"

"I can readily picture you chasing beetles, but I can't see you chasing fairies at all," she asserted positively.

"Nor can I. If you chase them, they vanish. Every one knows that."

"Anyway, your orchids were fit for a fairy queen. I haven't thanked you for them yet."

"Indeed you have. Much more than they deserve. By coming here to-day."

"Oh, that was a point of honor. Are you going to let those lovely purple ones wither on that prickly plant down there? Think how much better they'd look pinned on me - if there were any one here to see and appreciate."

If this were a hint, it failed of its aim, for, as the hermit scuttled out from his shelter, looking not unlike some bulky protrusive-eyed insect, secured the orchids, and returned, he never once glanced up. Safe again in his rock-bound retreat, he spoke: -

"'Rapunzel, Rapunzel, let down your hair.'"

"So you do know something of fairies and fairy lore!" she cried.

"Oh, it wasn't much more than a hundred years ago that I read my Grimm. In the story, only one call was necessary."

"Well, I can't spare any more of my silken tresses. I brought a string this time. Where's the other hair line?"

"I've used it to tether a fairy thought so that it can't fly away from me. Draw up slowly."

"Thank you so much, and I'm so glad that you are feeling better."

"Better?"

"Yes. Better than the day before yesterday."

"Day before yesterday?"

"Bless the poor man! Much anxious waiting hath bemused his wits. He thinks he's an echo."

"But I was all right the day before yesterday."

"You weren't. You were a prey to the most thrilling terrors. You were a moving picture of tender masculinity in distress. You let bashfulness like a worm i' th' bud prey upon your damask cheek. Have you a damask cheek? Stand out! I wish to consider you impartially. YOU needn't look at ME, you know."

"I'm not going to," he assured her, stepping forth obediently.

"Basilisk that I am!" she laughed. "How brown you are! How long did you say you'd been here? A year?"

"Fourteen weary Voiceless months. Not on this island, you know, but around the tropics."

"Yet you look vigorous and alert; not like the men I've seen come back from the hot countries, all languid and worn out. And you do look clean."

"Why shouldn't I be clean?"

"Of course you should. But people get slack, don't they, when they live off all alone by themselves? Still, I suppose you spruced up a little for me?"

"Nothing of the sort," he denied, with heat.

"No? Oh, my poor little vanity! He wouldn't dress up for us, Vanity, though we did dress up for him, and we're looking awfully nice - for a voice, that is. Do you always keep so soft and pink and smooth, Mr. Beetle Man?"

"I own a razor, if that's what you mean. You're making fun of me. Well, *I* don't mind." He lifted his voice and chanted: -

    "Although beyond the pale of law,

He always kept a polished jaw;
For he was one of those who saw
A saving hope
In shaving soap."

"Oh, lovely! What a noble finish. What is it?"

"Extract from 'Biographical Blurbings.'"

"Autobiographical?"

"Yes. By Me."

"And are you beyond the pale of law?"

"Poetical license," he explained airily. "Hold on, though." He fell silent a moment, and out of that silence came a short laugh. "I suppose I AM beyond the pale of law, now that I come to think of it. But you needn't be alarmed, I'm not a really dangerous criminal."

Later she was to recall that confession with sore misgivings. Now she only inquired lightly:

"Is that why you ran away from the tram car yesterday?" "Ran away? I didn't run away," he said, with dignity. "It just happened that there came into my mind an important engagement that I'd forgotten. My memory isn't what it should be. So I just turned over the matter in hand to an acquaintance of mine."

"The matter in hand being me."

"Why, yes; and the acquaintance being Mr. Cluff. I saw him throw four men out of a hotel once for insulting a girl, so I knew that he was much better at that sort of thing than I. May I go back now and sit down?" "Of course. I don't know whether I ought to thank you about yesterday or be very angry. It was such an extraordinary performance on your part -"

"Nothing extraordinary about it." His voice came up out of the shadow, full of judicial confidence. "Merely sound common sense."

"To leave a woman who has been insulted -"

"In more competent hands than one's own."

"Oh, I give it up!" she cried. "I don't understand you at all. Fitzhugh is right; you haven't a tradition to your name."

"Tradition," he repeated thoughtfully. "Why, I don't know. They're pretty rigid things, traditions. Rusty in the joints and all that sort of thing. Life isn't a process of machinery, exactly. One has to meet it with something more supple and adjustable than traditions."

"Is that your philosophy? Suppose a man struck you. Wouldn't you hit him back?"

"Perhaps. It would depend."

"Or insulted your country? Don't you believe that men should be ready to die, if necessary, in such a cause?"

"Some men. Soldiers, for instance. They're paid to."

"Good Heavens! Is it all a question of pay in your mind? Wouldn't YOU, unless you were paid for it?"

"How can I tell until the occasion arises?"

"Are you afraid?"

"I suppose I might be."

"Hasn't the man any blood in his veins?" cried his inquisitor, exasperated. "Haven't you ever been angry clear through?"

"Oh, of course; and sorry for it afterward. One is likely to lose one's temper any time. It might easily happen to me and drive me to make a fool of myself, like - like -" His voice trailed off into a silence of embarrassment.

"Like Fitzhugh Carroll. Why not say it? Well, I much prefer him and his hot-headedness to you and your careful wisdom."

"Of course," he acquiesced patiently. "Any girl would. It's the romantic temperament."

"And yours is the scientific, I suppose. That doesn't take into account little things like patriotism and heroism, does it? Tell me, have you actually ever admired - really got a thrill out of - any deed of heroism?"

"Oh, yes," he replied tranquilly. "I've done my bit of hero worship in my time. In fact, I've never quite recovered from it."

"No! Really? Do go on. You're growing more human every minute."

"Do you happen to know anything about the Havana campaign?"

"Not much. It never seemed to me anything to brag of. Dad says the Spanish-American War grew a crop of newspaper-made heroes, manufactured by reporters who really took more risks and showed more nerve than the men they glorified."

"Spanish-American War? That isn't what I'm talking about. I'm speaking of Walter Reed and his fellow scientists, who went down there and fought the mosquitoes."

The girl's lip curled.

"So that's your idea of heroism! Scrubby peckers into the lives of helpless bugs!"

"Have you the faintest idea what you are talking about?"

His voice had abruptly hardened. There was an edge to it; such an edge as she had faintly heard on the previous night, when Carroll had pressed him too hard. She was startled.

"Perhaps I haven't," she admitted.

"Then it's time you learned. Three American doctors went down into that pesthole of a Cuban city to offer their lives for a theory. Not for a tangible fact like the flag, or for glory and fame as in battle, but for a theory that might or might not be true. There wasn't a day or a night that their lives weren't at stake. Carroll let himself be bitten by infected mosquitoes on a final test, and grazed death by a hair's breadth. Lazear was bitten at his work, and died in the agony of yellow-fever convulsions, a martyr and a hero if ever there was one. Because of them, Havana is safe and livable now. We were able to build the Panama Canal because of their work, their - what did you call it? - scrubby peeking into the lives of -"

"Don't!" cried the girl. "I - I'm ashamed. I didn't know."

"How should you?" he said, in a changed tone. "We Americans set up monuments to our destroyers, not to our preservers, of life. Nobody knows about Walter Reed and James Carroll and Jesse Lazear - not even the American Government, which they officially served - except a few doctors and dried-up entomologists like myself. Forgive me. I didn't mean to deliver a lecture."

There was a long pause, which she broke with an effort.

"Mr. Beetle Man?"

"Yes, Voice?"

"I - I'm beginning to think you rather more man than beetle at times."

"Well, you see, you touched me on a point of fanaticism," he apologized.

"Do you mind standing up again for examination? No," she decided, as he stepped out and stood with his eyes lowered obstinately. "You don't seem changed to outward view. You still remind me," with a ripple of irrepressible laughter, "of a near-sighted frog. It's those ridiculous glasses. Why do you wear them?"

"To keep the sun out of my eyes."

"And the moon at night, I suppose. They're not for purposes of disguise?"

"Disguise! What makes you say that?" he asked quickly.

"Don't bark. They'd be most effective. And they certainly give your face a truly weird expression, in addition to its other detriments."

"If you don't like my face, consider my figure," he suggested optimistically. "What's the matter with that?"

"Stumpy," she pronounced. "You're all in a chunk. It does look like a practical sort of a chunk, though."

"Don't you like it?" he asked anxiously.

"Oh, well enough of its kind." She lifted her voice and chanted: -

"He was stubby and square,
But SHE didn't much care.

"There's a verse in return for yours. Mine's adapted, though. Examination's over. Wait. Don't sit down. Now, tell me your opinion of me."

"Very musical."

"I'm not musical at all."

"Oh, I'm considering you as a VOICE."

"I'm tired of being just a voice. Look up here. Do," she pleaded. "Turn upon me those lucent goggles."

>*When orbs like thine the soul disclose,*
>*Tee-deedle-deedle-dee.*

Don't be afraid. One brief fleeting glance ere we part."

"No," he returned positively. "Once is enough."

"On behalf of my poor traduced features, I thank you humbly. Did they prove as bad as you feared?"

"Worse. I've hardly forgotten yet what you look like. Your kind of face is bad for business."

"What is business?"

"Haven't I told you? I'm a scientist."

"Well, I'm a specimen. No beetle that crawls or creeps or hobbles, or does whatever beetles are supposed to do, shows any greater variation from type - I heard a man say that in a lecture once - than I do. Can't I interest you in my case, O learned one? The proper study of mankind is -"

"Woman. Yes, I know all about that. But I'm a groundling."

"Mr. Beetle Man," she said, in a tremulous voice, "the rock is moving."

"I don't feel it. Though it might be a touch of earthquake. We have 'em often."

"Not your rock. The tarantula rock, I mean."

"Nonsense! A hundred tarantulas couldn't stir it."

"Well, it seems to be moving, and that's just as bad. I'm tired and I'm lonely. Oh, please, Professor Scarab, have I got to fall on your neck again to introduce a little human companionship into this conversation?"

"Caesar! No! My shoulder's still lame. What do you want, anyway?"

"I want to know about you and your work. ALL about you."

"Humph! Well, at present I'm making some microscopical studies of insects. That's the reason for these glasses. The light is so harsh in these latitudes that it affects the vision a trifle, and every trifle counts in microscopy."

"Does the microscope add charm to the beetle?"

"Some day I'll show you, if you like. Just now it's the flea, the national bird of Caracuna."

"The wicked flea?"

"Nobody knows how wicked until he has studied him on his native heath."

"Doesn't the flea have something to do with plague? They say there's plague in the city now. You knew all about the Dutch. Do you know anything about the plague?"

"You've been listening to bolas."

"What's a bola?"

"A bola is information that somebody who is totally ignorant of the facts whispers confidentially in your ear with the assurance that he knows it to be authentic - in other words, a lie."

"Then there isn't any plague down under those quaint, old, red-tiled roofs?"

"Who ever knows what's going on under those quaint, old, red-tiled roofs? No foreigner, certainly."

"Even I can feel the mystery, little as I've seen of the place," said the girl.

"Oh, that's the Indian of it. The tiled roofs are Spanish; the speech is Spanish; but just beneath roof and speech, the life and thought are profoundly and unfathomably Indian."

"Not with all the Caracunans, surely. Take Mr. Raimonda, for instance."

"Ah, that's different. Twenty families of the city, perhaps, are pure-bloods. There are no finer, cleaner fellows anywhere than the well-bred Caracunans. They are men of the world, European educated, good sportsmen, straight, honorable gentlemen. Unfortunately not they, but a gang of mongrel grafters control the politics of the country."

"For a hermit of science, you seem to know a good deal of what goes on. By the way, Mr. Raimonda called on me - on us last evening."

"So he mentioned. Rather serious, that, you know."

"Far from it. He was very amusing."

"Doubtless," commented the other dryly. "But it isn't fair to play the game with one who doesn't know the rules. Besides, what will Mr. Preston Fairfax - "

"For a professedly shy person, you certainly take a rather intimate tone."

"Oh, I'm shy only under the baleful influence of the feminine eye. Besides, you set the note of intimacy when you analyzed my personal appearance. And finally, I have a warm regard for young Raimonda."

"So have I," she returned maliciously. "Aren't you jealous?"

He laughed.

"Please be a little bit jealous. It would be so flattering."

"Jealousy is another tradition in which I don't believe."

"Then I can't flirt with you at all?" she sighed. "After taking all this long hot walk to see you!"

PLOP! The sound punctured the silence sharply, though not loudly. Some large fruit pod bursting on a distant tree might have made such a report.

"What was that?" asked the girl curiously.

"That? Oh, that was a revolver shot," he remarked.

"Aren't you casual! Do revolver shots mean nothing to you?"

"That one shakes my soul's foundations." His tone by no means indicated an inner cataclysm. "It may mean that I must excuse myself and leave. Just a moment, please."

Passing across the line of her vision, he disappeared to the left. When she next heard his voice, it was almost directly above her.

"No," it said. "There's no hurry. The flag's not up."

"What flag?"

"The flag in my compound."

"Can you see your home from here?"

"Yes; there's a ledge on the cliff that gives a direct view."

"I want to come up and see it."

"You can't. It's much too hard a climb. Besides, there are rock devilkins on the way."

"And when you hear a shot, you go up there for messages?"

"Yes; it's my telephone system."

"Who's at the other end?"

"The peon who pretends to look after the quinta for me."

"A man! No man can keep a house fit to live in," she said scornfully.

"I know it; but he's all I've got in the servant line."

"How far is the house from here?"

"A mile, by air. Seven by trail from town."

"Isn't it lonely?"

"Yes."

Suddenly she felt very sorry for him. There was such a quiet, conclusive acceptance of cheerlessness in the monosyllable.

"How soon must you go back?"

"Oh, not for an hour, at least."

"If it's a call, it must be an important one, so far from civilization."

"Not necessarily. Don't you ever have calls that are not important?"

No answer came.

"Miss Brewster!" he called. "Oh, Voice! You haven't gone?"

Still no response.

"That isn't fair," he complained, making his way swiftly down, and satisfying himself by a peep about the angle commanding her point of the rock that she had, indeed, vanished. Sadly he descended to his own nook - and jumped back with a half-suppressed yell.

"You needn't jump out of your skin on my account," said Miss Polly Brewster, with a gracious smile. "I'm not a devilkin."

"You are! That is - I mean - I - I - beg your pardon. I - I -"

"The poor man's having another bashful fit," she observed, with malicious glee. "Did the bold, bad, forward American minx scare it almost out of its poor shy wits?"

"You - you startled me."

"No!" she exclaimed, in wide-eyed mock surprise. "Who would have supposed it? You didn't expect me down here, did you?"

Thereupon she got a return shock.

"Yes, I did," he said; "sooner or later."

"Don't fib. Don't pretend that you knew I was here."

"W-w-well, no. Not just now. B-b-but I knew you'd come if - if - if I pretended I didn't want you to long enough."

"Young and budding scientist," said she severely, "you're a gay deceiver. Is it because you have known me in some former existence that you are able thus accurately to read my character?"

"Well, I knew you wouldn't stay up there much longer."

"I'm angry at you; very angry at you. That is, I would be if it weren't that you really didn't mean it when you said that you really didn't want to see my face again."

"Did any one ever see your face once without wanting to see it again?"

"Ah, bravo!" She clapped her hands gayly. "Marvelous improvement under my tutelage! Where, oh, where is your timidity now?"

"I - I - I forgot," he stammered, "As long as I don't think, I'm all right. Now, you - you - you've gone and spoiled me."

"Oh, the pity of it! Let's find some mild, impersonal topic, then, that won't embarrass you. What do you do under the shadow of this rock, in a parched land?"

"Work. Besides, it isn't a parched land. Look on this side."

Half a dozen steps brought her around the farther angle, where, hidden in a growth of shrubbery, lay a little pool of fairy loveliness,

"That's my outdoor laboratory."

"A dreamery, I'd call it. May I sit down? Are there devilkins here? There's an elfkin, anyway," she added, as a silvered dragon-fly hovered above her head inquisitively before darting away on his own concerns.

"One of my friends and specimens. I'm studying his methods of aviation with a view to making some practical use of what I learn, eventually."

"Really? Are you an inventor, too? I'm crazy about aviation."

"Ah, then you'll be interested in this," he said, now quite at his ease. "You know that the mosquito is the curse of the tropics."

"Of other places, as well."

"But in the tropics it means yellow fever, Chagres fever, and other epidemic illness. Now, the mosquito, as you doubtless realize, is a monoplane."

"A monoplane?" repeated the girl, in some puzzlement. "How a monoplane?"

"I thought you claimed some knowledge of aviation. Its wings are all on one plane. The great natural enemy of the mosquito is the dragon-fly, one of which just paid you a visit. Now, modern warfare has taught us that the most effective assailant of the monoplane is a biplane. You know that."

"Y-y-yes," said the girl doubtfully.

"Therefore, if we can breed a biplane dragonfly in sufficient numbers, we might solve the mosquito problem at small expense."

"I don't know much about science," she began, "but I should hardly have supposed -"

"It's curious how nature varies the type of aviation," he continued dreamily. "Now, the pigeon is, of course, a Zeppelin; whereas the sea urchin is obviously a balloon; and the thistledown an undirigible -"

"You're making fun of me!" she accused, with sharp enlightenment.

"What else have you done to me ever since we met?" he inquired mildly.

"Now I AM angry! I shall go home at once."

A second far-away PLOP! set a period to her decision.

"So shall I," said he briskly.

"Does that signal mean hurry up?" she asked curiously.

"Well, it means that I'm wanted. You go first. When will you come again?"

"Not at all."

"Do you mean that?"

"Of course. I'm angry. Didn't I tell you that? I don't permit people to make fun of me. Besides, you must come and see me next. You owe me two calls. Will you?"

"I - I - don't know."

"Afraid?"

"Rather."

"Then you must surely come and conquer this cowardice. Will you come to-morrow?"

"No; I don't think so."

Miss Brewster opened wide her eyes upon him. She was little accustomed to have her invitations, which she issued rather in the manner of royal commands, thus casually received. Had the offender been any other of her acquaintance, she would have dropped the matter and the man then and there. But this was a different species. Graceful and tactful he might not be, but he was honest.

"Why?" she said.

"I've got something more important to do."

"You're reverting to type sadly. What is it that's so important?"

"Work."

"You can work any time."

"No. Unfortunately I have to eat and sleep sometimes."

The implication she accepted quite seriously.

" Are you really as busy as all that? I'm quite

conscience-stricken over the time I've wasted for you."

"Not wasted at all. You've cheered me up."

"That's something. But you won't come to the city to be cheered up?"

"Yes, I will. When I get time."

"Perhaps you won't find me at home."

"Then I'll wait."

"Good-bye, then," she laughed, "until your leisure day arrives."

She climbed the rock, stepping as strongly and surely as a lithe animal. At the top, the spirit of roguery, ever on her lips and eyes, struck in and possessed her soul.

"O disciple of science!" she called.

"Well?"

"Can you see me?"

"Not from here."

"Good! I'm a Voice again. So don't be timid. Will you answer a question?"

"I've answered a hundred already. One more won't hurt."

"Have you ever been in love?"

Samuel Hopkins Adams

"What?"

"Don't I speak plainly enough? Have - you - ever - been - in - love?"

"With a woman?"

"Why, yes," she railed. "With a woman, of course. I don't mean with your musty science."

"No."

"Well, you needn't be violent. Have you ever been in love with ANYTHING?"

"Perhaps."

"Oh, perhaps!" she taunted. "There are no perhapses in that. With what?"

"With what every man in the world is in love with once in his life," he replied thoughtfully.

She made a little still step forward and peeped down at him. He stood leaning against the face of the rock, gazing out over the hot blue Caribbean, his hat pushed back and his absurd goggles firm and high on his nose. His words and voice were in preposterous contrast to his appearance.

"Riddle me your riddle," she commanded. "What is every man in love with once in his life?"

"An ideal."

"Ah! And your ideal - where do you keep it safe from

the common gaze?"

"I tether it to my heart - with a single hair," said the man below.

"Oh," commented Miss Brewster, in a changed tone. And, again, "Oh," just a little blankly. "I wish I hadn't asked that," she confessed silently to herself, after a moment.

Still, the spirit of reckless experimentalism pressed her onward.

"That's a peril to the scientific mind, you know," she warned. "Suppose your ideal should come true?"

"It won't," said he comfortably.

Miss Brewster's regrets sensibly mitigated.

"In that case, of course, your career is safe from accident," she remarked.

He moved out into the open.

"Mr. Beetle Man," she called,

He looked up and saw her with her chin cupped in her hand, regarding him thoughtfully.

"I'm NOT just a casual acquaintance," she said suddenly. "That is, if you don't want me to be."

"That's good," was his hearty comment. "I'm glad you like me better than you did at first."

"Oh, I'm not so sure that I like you, exactly. But I'm coming to have a sort of respectful curiosity about you. What lies under that beetle shell of yours, I wonder?" she mused, in a half breath.

Whether or not he heard the final question she could not tell. He smiled, waved his hand, and disappeared. Below, she watched the motion of the bush-tops where the shrubbery was parted by the progress of his sturdy body down the long slope.

V

AN UPHOLDER OF TRADITIONS

One day passes much like another in Caracuna City. The sun rises blandly, grows hot and angry as it climbs the slippery polished vault of the heavens, and coasts down to its rest in a pleased and mild glow. From the squat cathedral tower the bells clang and jangle defiance to the Adversary, temporarily drowning out the street tumult in which the yells of the lottery venders, the braying of donkeys, the whoops of the cabmen, and the blaring of the little motor cars with big horns, combine to render Caracuna the noisiest capital in the world. Through the saddle-colored hordes on the moot ground of the narrow sidewalks moves an occasional Anglo-Saxon resident, browned and sallowed, on his way to the government concession that he manages; a less occasional Anglo-Saxoness, browned and marked with the seal that the tropics put upon every woman who braves their rigors for more than a brief period; and a sprinkling of tourists in groups, flying on cheek, brow, and nose the stark red of their newness to the climate.

Not of this sorority Miss Polly Brewster. Having blithe regard to her duty as an ornament of this dull world, she had tempered the sun to the foreign cuticle with successively diminishing layers of veils, to such good purpose that the celestial scorcher had but kissed her graduated brownness to a soft glow of color. Not alone in appreciation of her external advantages was Miss Brewster. Such as it was, - and it had its qualities, albeit somewhat unformulated, - Caracuna society gave her prompt welcome. There were teas and rides and tennis at the little club; there were agreeable, presentable men and hospitable women; and always there was Fitzhugh Carroll, suave, handsome, gentle, a polished man of the world among men, a courteous attendant to every woman, but always with a first thought for her. Was it sheer perversity of character, that elfin perversity so shrewdly divined by the hermit of the mountain, that put in her mind, in this far corner of the world, among these strange people, the thought:

"All men are alike, and Fitz, for all that he's so different and the best of them, is the MOST alike."

Which paradox, being too much for her in the heat of the day, she put aside in favor of the insinuating thought of her beetle man. Whatever else he might or might not be, he wasn't alike. She was by no means sure that she found this difference either admirable or amiable. But at least it was interesting.

Moreover, she was piqued. For four days had passed and the recluse had not returned her call. True, there had come to her hotel a wicker full of superb wild tree blooms, and, again, a tiny box, cunning in workmanship of scented wood, containing what at first glance she had taken to be a jewel, until she saw that it was a tiny butterfly with opalescent wings, mounted on a silver wire. But with them had come no word or token of identification. Perhaps they weren't from the queer and remote person at all. Very likely Mr. Raimonda had sent them; or Fitzhugh Carroll was adding secret attention to his open homage; or they might even be a further peace offering from the Hochwald secretary.

That occasionally too festive diplomat had, indeed, made amends both profound and, evidently, sincere. Soliciting the kind offices of both Sherwen and Raimonda, he had presented himself, under their escort, stiff and perspiring in his full official regalia, before Mr. Brewster; then before his daughter, whose solemnity, presently breaking down before his painfully rehearsed English, dissolved in fluent French, setting him at ease and making him her slave. Poor penitent Von Plaanden even apologized to Carroll, fortunately not having heard of the American's threat, and made a most favorable impression upon that precisian.

"Intoxicated, he may be a rough, Miss Polly," Carroll confided to the girl. "But sober, the man is a gentleman. He feels very badly about the whole affair. Offered to your father to report it all through official channels and attach his resignation."

"Not for worlds!" cried Miss Polly. "The poor man was half asleep. And Mr. Bee - Mr. Perkins DID jog him rather sharply."

"Yes. Von Plaanden asked my advice as an American about his attitude toward Cluff and Perkins."

"I hope you told him to let the whole thing drop."

"Exactly what I did. I explained about Cluff; that he was a very good fellow, but of a different class, and probably wouldn't give the thing another thought."

"And Mr. Perkins?"

"Von Plaanden wanted to challenge him, if he could find him. I suggested that he leave me to deal with Mr. Perkins. After some discussion, he agreed."

"Oh! And what are you going to do with him?"

"Find him first, if I can."

"I can tell you where." Carroll stared at her, astonished. "But I don't think I will."

"He announced his intention of keeping out of my way. The man has no sense of shame."

"You probably scared the poor lamb out of his wits, fire-eater that you are."

Carroll would have liked to think so, but an innate sense of justice beneath his crust of prejudice forbade him to accept this judgment.

"The strange part of it is that he doesn't impress me as being afraid. But there is certainly something very wrong with the fellow. A man who will deliberately desert a woman in distress" - Carroll's manner expanded into the roundly rhetorical - "whatever else he may be, cannot be a gentleman."

"There might have been mitigating circumstances."

"No circumstances could excuse such an action. And, after that, the fellow had the effrontery to send you a message."

"Me? What was it?" asked Miss Polly quickly.

"I don't know. I didn't let him finish. I forbade his even mentioning your name."

"Indeed!" cried the girl, in quick dudgeon. "Don't you think you are taking a great deal upon yourself, Fitz? What do you really know about Mr. Perkins, anyway, that you judge him so offhandedly?"

"Very little, but enough, I think. And I hardly think you know more."

"Then you're wrong. I do."

"You KNOW this man?"

"Yes; I do."

"Does your father approve of -"

"Never mind my father! He has confidence enough in me to let me judge of my own friends."

"Friends?" Carroll's handsome face clouded and reddened. "If I had known that he was a friend of yours, Miss Polly, I never would have spoken as I did. I'm most sincerely sorry," he added, with grave courtesy.

The girl's color deepened under the brown.

"He isn't exactly a friend," she admitted. "I've just met and talked with him a few times. But your judgment seemed so unfair, on such a slight basis."

"I'm sorry I can't reverse my judgment," said the Southerner stiffly, "But I know of only one standard for those matters."

"That's just your trouble." Her eyes took on a cold gleam as she scanned the perfection and finish of the man before her. "Fitzhugh, do you wear ready-made clothing?"

"Of course not," he answered, in surprise at this turn.

"Your suits are all made to order?"

"Yes, Miss Polly."

"And your shirts?"

"Yes, and shoes, and various other things." He smiled.

"Why do you have them specially made?"

"Beeause they suit me better, and I can afford it."

"It's really because you want them individualized for you, isn't it?"

"Yes; I suppose so."

"Then why do you always get your mental clothes ready-made?"

"I don't think I understand, Miss Polly," he said gently.

"It seems to me that all your ideas and estimates and standards are of stock pattern," she explained relentlessly. "Inside, you're as just exactly so as a pair of wooden shoes. Can't you see that you can't judge all men on the same plane?"

"I see that you're angry with me, and I see that I'm being punished for what I said about - about Mr. Perkins. If I'd known that you took any interest in him, I'd have bitten my tongue in two before speaking as I did. As for the message, if you wish it, I'll go to him -"

"Oh, that doesn't matter," she interrupted.

"This much I can say, in honesty," continued the Southerner, with an effort: "I had a talk, almost an encounter, with him in the plaza, and I don't believe he is the coward I thought him."

His intent to be fair to the object of his scorn was so genuine that his critic felt a swift access of compunction.

"Oh, Fitz," she said sweetly, "you're not to blame. I should have told you. And you're honest and loyal and a gentleman. Only I wish sometimes that you weren't quite so awfully gentlemanly a gentleman."

The Southerner made a gesture of despair.

"If I could only understand you, Miss Polly!"

"Don't hope it. I've never yet understood myself. But there's a sympathy in me for the under dog, and this Mr. Perkins seems a sort of helpless creature. Yet in another way he doesn't seem helpless at all. Quite the reverse. Oh, dear! I'm tired of Perkins, Perkins, Perkins! Let's talk about something pleasanter - like the plague."

"What's that about Perkins'?" Galpy had entered the drawing-room where the conversation had been carried on, and now crossed over to them. "I'll tell you a good one on the little blighteh. D' you know what they call him at the Club Amicitia since his adventure on the street car, Miss Brewster?"

"What?"

"'The Unspeakable Perk.' Rippin', ain't it? Like 'The Unspeakable Turk,' you know."

Despite herself, Polly's lips twitched; in some ways he WAS unspeakable.

"They've nicknamed him that because of his trying to help me, and then - leaving?" she asked.

"Oh, not entirely. There's other things. He's a nahsty, stand-offish way with him, you know. Don't-want-to-know-yeh trick. Wouldn't-speak-to-yeh-if-I-could-help-it twist to his face. 'The Unspeakable Perk.' Stands him right, I should say. There's other reasons, too."

"What are they?"

She saw a quick, warning frown on Carroll's sharply turned face. Galpy noted it, too, and was lost in confusion.

"Oh - ah - just gossip - nothing at all. I say, Miss Brewster, the railway - I'm in the Ferrocarril-del-Norte office, you know - has offered your party a special on an hour's notice, any time you want it."

"That's most kind of your road, Mr. Galpy. But why should we want it?"

"Things might be getting a bit ticklish any day now. I've just taken the message from the manager to your father."

The young Englishman took his leave, and Polly Brewster went to her room, to freshen up for luncheon, carrying with her the sobriquet she had just heard. Certainly, applied to its subject, it had a mucilaginous consistency. It stuck.

"'The Unspeakable Perk,'" she repeated, with a little chuckle. "If I had a month to train him in, eh, what a speakable Perk I'd make him! I'd make him into a Perk that would sit up and speak when I lifted my little finger." She considered this. "I'm not so sure," she concluded, more doubtfully. "How can one tell through those horrid glasses, particularly when one doesn't see him for days and days?"

Without moving, she might, however, have seen him forthwith, for at that precise and particular moment, the Unspeakable Perk was in plain sight of her window, on a bench in the corner of the plaza, engaged in light conversation with a legless and philosophical beggar whom he had just astonished by the presentation of a whole bolivar, of the value of twenty cents gold.

After she had finished luncheon and returned to her room, he was still there. Not until the mid-heat of the afternoon, however, did she observe, first with puzzlement, then with a start of recognition, the patiently rounded brown back of the forward-leaning figure in the corner. Greatly wroth was Miss Polly Brewster. For some hours - two, at least - the man to keep tryst and wager with whom she had tramped up miles of mountain road had been in town and hadn't called upon her! Truly was he an Unspeakable Perk!

Wasn't there possibly a mistake somewhere, though? A second peep at the far-away back interpreted into the curve a suggestion of resigned waiting. Maybe he had called, after all. Thought being usually with Miss Brewster the mother of the twins, Determination and Action, she slipped downstairs and inquired of the three guardians of the door, in such Spanish as she could muster, whether a Mr. Perkins, wearing large glasses - this in the universal sign manual - had been to see her that day.

"Si, Senorita" - he had.

Why, then, hadn't his name been brought to her?

Extended hands and up-shrugged shoulders that might mean either apology or incomprehension.

Straightway Miss Brewster pinned a hat upon her brown head at an altogether casual and heart-distracting angle and sallied down into the tesselated bowl of the park. Quite unconscious of her approach, until she was close upon him, her objective chatted fluently with the legless one, until she spoke quietly, almost in his ear. Then it was only by a clutch at the bench back that he saved himself from disaster on his return to earth.

"Wh - wh - what - wh - where - how did you come here?" he stuttered.

"Now, now, don't be alarmed," she admonished. "Shut your eyes, draw a deep breath, count three. And, as soon as you are ready I'll give you a talisman against social panic. Are you ready?"

"Y-yes."

"Very well. Whenever I come upon you suddenly, you mustn't try to jump up into a tree as you did just now -"

"I didn't!"

"Oh, yes. Or burrow under a rock, as you did the other day -"

"Miss B-B-Brewster -"

"Wait until I've finished. You must turn your thoughts firmly upon your science, until you've recovered equilibrium and the power of human speech."

"But when you jump at me that way, I c-c-can't think of anything but you."

"That's where the charm comes in. As soon as you see me or hear me approaching, you must repeat, quite slowly, this scientific incantation." She beat time with a pink and rhythmic finger as she chanted: -

   "*Scarab, tarantula, doodle-bug, flea.*"

The beggar rapidly made the sign that protects one from the influence of the malign and supernatural. The scientist scowled.

"Repeat it!" she commanded.

"There is no such insect as a doodle-bug," he protested feebly.

"Isn't there? I thought I heard you mention it in your conversation with Mr. Carroll the other night."

"You put that into my head," he accused.

"Truly? Then life is indeed real and earnest. To have introduced something unscientific into that compendium of science - there's triumph enough for any ambition. Besides, see how beautifully it scans."

Again she beat time, and again the beggar crooked defensive fingers as she declaimed: -

"SCAR-ab, tar-ANT-u-la, DOO-dle-bug, FLEA!"

Homeric, I call it. Perhaps you think you could improve on it."

"Would you mind substituting 'neuropter' in the third strophe?" he ventured. "It would be just as good as 'doodle-bug,' and more - more accurate."

"What's a neuropter? You didn't make him up for the occasion?"

"Heaven forbid! The dragon-fly is a neuropter. The dragon-fly we're going to breed to a biplane, you know," he reminded her slyly.

"Indeed! Well, I shall stick to my doodle-bug. He's more euphonious. Now, repeat it."

"Let me off this time," he pleaded. "I'm all right - quite recovered. It's only at the start that it's so bad."

"Very well," she agreed. "But you're not to forget it. And next time we meet you're to be sure and say it over until you're sane."

"Sane!" he said resentfully. "I'm as sane as any one you know. It's the job of KEEPING sane in this madhouse of the tropics that's almost driven me crazy."

"Lovely!" she approved. "Well, now that you've recovered, I'll tell you what I came out to say. I'm sorry that I missed you."

"Missed me?" he repeated. "Oh, you have missed me, then? That's nice. You see, I've been so busy for the last three or four days -"

"No; I haven't missed you a bit," she declared indignantly. "The conceit of the man!"

"But you said you w-w-were sorry you'd -"

"Don't be wholly a beetle! I meant I was sorry not to see you when you came to call on me this morning."

"I didn't come to call on you this morning."

"No? The boy at the door said he'd seen you, or something answering to your description."

"So he did. I came to see your father. He was out."

"What time?"

"From eleven on."

"Father? No, I don't think so."

"His secretary came down and told me so, or sent word each time."

She smiled pityingly at him.

"Of course. That's what a secretary is for."

"To tell lies?"

"White lies. You see, dad is a very busy man, and an important man, and many people come to see him whom he hasn't time to see. So, unless he knew your business, he would naturally be 'out' to you."

The corners of the young man's rather sensitive mouth flattened out perceptibly.

"Ah, I see. My mistake. Living in countries where, however queer the people may be, they at least observe ordinary human courtesies, one forgets - if one ever knew."

"What did you want of dad?"

"Oh, to borrow four dollars of him, of course," he replied dryly.

"You needn't be angry at me. You see, dad's time is valuable."

"Indeed? To whom?"

"Why, to himself, of course."

"Oh, well, my time - However, that doesn't matter. I haven't wholly wasted it." He glanced toward the beggar, who was profoundly regarding the cathedral clock.

"If you like, I'll get you an interview with dad," she offered magnanimously.

"Me? No, I thank you," he said crisply. "I'm not patient of unnecessary red tape."

Miss Brewster looked at him in surprise. It was borne in upon her, as she looked, that this man was not accustomed to being lightly regarded by other men, however busy or important; that his own concerns in life were quite as weighty to him, and in his esteem, perhaps, to others, as were the interests of any magnate; and that, man to man, there would be no shyness or indecision or purposelessness anywhere in his make-up.

"If it was important," she began hesitantly, "my father would be -"

"It was of no importance to me," he cut in. "To others - Perhaps I could see some one else of your party."

"Well, here I am." She smiled. "Why won't I do?"

Behind the obscuring disks she could feel his glance read her. The grimness at the mouth's corners relaxed.

"I really don't know why you shouldn't."

"Dad says I'd have made a man of affairs," she remarked.

"Why, it's just this. You should be planning to leave this country."

Miss Brewster bewailed her harsh lot with drooping lip.

"Every one wants to drive me away!"

"Who else?"

"That railroad man, Mr. Galpy, was offering us special inducements to leave, in the form of special trains any time we liked. It isn't hospitable."

"A jail is hospitable. But one doesn't stay in it when one can get out."

"If Caracuna were the jail and I the 'one,' one might. I quite love it here."

He made a sharp gesture of annoyance.

"Don't be childish," he said.

"Childish? You come down like Freedom from the mountain heights, and unfurl your warnings to the air, and complain of lost time and all that sort of thing, and what does it all amount to?" she demanded, with spirit. "That we should sail away, when you know perfectly well that the Dutch won't let us sail away! Childish, indeed! Don't you be BEETLISH!"

"There's a way out, without much risk, but some

discomfort. You could strike south-east to the Bird Reefs, take a small boat, and get over to the mainland. As soon as the blockade is off, the yacht can take your luggage around. The trip would be rough for you, but not dangerous. Not as dangerous as staying here may be."

"Do you really think it so serious?"

"Most emphatically."

"Will you come with us and show us the way?" she inquired, gazing with exaggerated appeal into his goggles.

"I? No."

"What shall you do?"

"Stick."

"Pins through scarabs," she laughed, "while beneath you Caracuna riots and revolutes and massacres foreigners. Nero with his fiddle was nothing to you."

"Miss Brewster, I'm afraid you are suffering from a misplaced sense of humor. Will you believe me when I tell you that I have certain sources of information in local matters both serviceable and reliable?"

"You seem to have bet on a certainty in the Dutch blockade matter."

"Well, it's equally certain that there is bubonic plague here."

"A bola. You told me so yourself."

"Perhaps there was nothing to be gained then by letting you know, as you were bottled up, with no way out. Now, through the good offices of a foreign official, who, of course, couldn't afford to appear, this opportunity to reach the mainland is open to you."

"Had you anything to do with that?" she inquired suspiciously.

"Oh, the official is a friend of mine," he answered carelessly.

"And you really believe that there is an epidemic of plague here? Don't you think that I'd make a good Red Cross nurse?"

His voice was grave and rather stern.

"You've never seen bubonic plague," he said, "or you wouldn't joke about it."

"I'm sorry. But it wasn't wholly a joke. If we were really cooped up with an epidemic, I'd volunteer. What else would there be to do?"

"Nothing of the sort," he cried vehemently. "You don't know what you're talking about."

"Anyway, isn't the wonderful Luther Pruyn on his way to exorcise the demon, or something of the sort?"

"What about Luther Pruyn? Who says he's coming here?"

"It's the gossip of the diplomatic set and the clubs. He's the favorite mystery of the day."

"Well, if he does come, it won't improve matters any, for the first case he verifies he'll clap on a quarantine that a mouse couldn't creep through. I know something of the Pruyn method."

"And don't wholly approve it, I judge."

"It may be efficacious, but it's extremely inconvenient at times."

Again the cathedral clock boomed.

"See how I've kept you from your own affairs!" cried Miss Polly contritely. "What are you going to do now? Go back to your mountains?"

"Yes. As soon as you tell me that your father will go out by the reefs."

"Do you expect him to make up his mind, on five minutes' notice, to abandon his yacht?"

"I thought great magnates were supposed to be men of instant and unalterable decisions. I don't know the type."

"Anyway, dad has gone out. I saw him drive away. Wouldn't to-morrow do?"

"Why, yes; I suppose so."

"I'll tell you. The Voice will report at the rock to-morrow, at four."

"No."

"What a very uncompromising 'no'!"

"I can't be there at four. Make it five."

"What a very arbitrary beetle man! Well, as I've wasted so much of your time to-day, I'll accept your orders for to-morrow."

"And please impress your father with the extreme advisability of your getting off this island."

"Yes, sir," she said meekly. "You'll be most awfully glad to get rid of us, won't you?"

"Very greatly relieved."

"And a little bit sorry?"

The begoggled face turned toward her. There was a perceptible tensity in the line of the jaw. But the beetle man made no answer.

"Now, if I could see behind those glasses," said Miss Polly Brewster to her wicked little self, "I'd probably BITE myself rather than say it again. Just the same - And a little bit sorry?" she persisted aloud.

"Does that matter?" said the man quietly.

Miss Polly Brewster forthwith bit herself on her pink and wayward tongue.

"Don't think I'm not grateful," she employed that chastened member to say. "I am, most deeply. So will father be, even if he decides not to leave. I'm afraid that's what he will decide."

"He mustn't."

"Tell him that yourself."

"I will, if it becomes necessary."

"Let me be present at the interview. Most people are afraid of dad. Perhaps you'd be, too."

"I could always run away," he remarked, unsmiling. "You know how well I do it."

"I must do it now myself, and get arrayed for the daily tea sacrifice. Au revoir."

"Hasta manana," he said absently.

She had turned to go, but at the word she came slowly back a pace or two, smiling.

"What a strange beetle man you are!" she said softly. "I have no other friends like you. You ARE a friend, aren't you, in your queer way?" She did not wait for an answer, but went on: "You don't come to see me when I ask you. You don't send me any word. You make me feel that, compared to your concerns with beetles and flies, I'm quite hopelessly unimportant. And yet here I find you giving up your own pursuits and wasting your time to plan and watch and think for us."

"For you," he corrected.

"For me," she accepted sweetly. "What an ungrateful

little pig you must think me! But truly inside I appreciate it and thank you, and I think - I feel that perhaps it amounts to a lot more than I know."

He made a gesture of negation.

"No great thing," he said. "But it's the best I can do, anyway. Do you remember what the mediaeval mummer said, when he came bearing his poor homage?"

"No. Tell it to me."

"It runs like this: 'Lady, who art nowise bitter to those who serve you with a good intent, that which thy servant is, that he is for you.'"

"Polly Brewster," said the girl to herself, as she walked, slowly and musingly, back to her room, "the busy haunts of men are more suited to your style than the free-and-untrammeled spaces of nature, and well you know it. But you'll go to-morrow and you'll keep on going until you find out what is behind those brown-green goblin spectacles. If only he didn't look so like a gnome!"

The clause conditional, introduced by the word "if," does not always imply a conclusion, even in the mind of the propounder. Miss Brewster would have been hard put to it to round out her subjunctive.

VI

FORKED TONGUES

"Pooh!" said Thatcher Brewster.

Thatcher Brewster's "Pooh!" is generally recognized in the realm of high finance as carrying weight. It is not derisive or contemptuous; it is dismissive. The subject of it simply ceases to exist. In the present instance, it was so mild as scarcely to stir the smoke from his after-dinner cigar, yet it had all the intent, if not the effect, of finality. The reason why it hadn't the effect was that it was directed at Thatcher Brewster's daughter.

"Perhaps not quite so much 'Pooh!' as you think," was that damsel's reception of the pregnant monosyllable.

"A bug-hunter from nowhere! Don't I know that type?" said the magnate, who confounded all scientists with inventors, the capital-seeking inventor being the bane and torment of his life.

"He knew about the Dutch blockade."

"Or pretended he did. I'm afraid my Pollipet has let herself romanticize a little."

"Romanticize!" The girl laughed. "If you could see him, dad! Romance and my poor little beetle man don't live in the same world."

Out of the realm of memory, where the echoes come and go by no known law, sounded his voice in her ear: "'That which thy servant is, that he is for you.'" Dim doubt forthwith began to cloud the bright certainty of Miss Brewster's verdict.

"If he's gone to all the trouble that I told you of, it must be that he has some good reason for wanting to get us safely out," she argued to her father.

"Perhaps he feels that his peace of mind would be more assured if you were in some other country," he teased. "No, my dear, I'm not leaving a full-manned yacht in a foreign harbor and smuggling myself out of a friendly country on the say-so of an unknown adviser, whose chief ability seems to lie in the hundred-yard dash."

"I think that's unfair and ungrateful. If a man with a sword -"

"When I begin a row, I stay with it," said Mr. Brewster grimly. "Quitters and I don't pull well together."

"Then I'm to tell him 'No'?"

"Positively."

"Not so positively at all. I shall say, 'No, thank you,' in my very nicest way, and say that you're very grateful and appreciative and not at all the growly old bear of a dad that you pretend to be when one doesn't know and love you. And perhaps I'll invite him to dine here and go away on the yacht with us -"

"And graciously accept a couple of hundred thousand dollars bonus, and come into the company as first vice-president," chuckled her father. "And then he'll wake up and find he's been sitting on a cactus. See here," he added, with a sharpening of tone, "do you suppose he could get a cablegram for transmission to Washington over to the mainland for us by this mysterious route of his?"

"Very likely."

"You're really sure you want to go, Pollipet? This is your cruise, you know."

"Yes, I do."

Hitherto Miss Polly had been declaring to all and sundry, including the beetle man himself, that it was her firm intent and pleasure to stay on the island and observe the presumptively interesting events that promised. That she had reversed this decision, on the unsolicited counsel of an extremely queer stranger, was a phenomenon the peculiarity of which did not strike her at the time. All that she felt was a settled confidence in the beetle man's sound reason for his advice.

"Very good," said Mr. Brewster. "If I can get through a message to the State Department, they'll bring pressure to bear on the Dutch, and we can take the yacht through the blockade. It's only a question of finding a way to lay the matter before the Dutch authorities, anyway. I've been making inquiries here, and I find there's no intention of bottling up neutral pleasure craft. I dare say we could get out now. Only it's possible that the Hollanders might shoot first and ask questions afterward."

"It would have to be done quickly, dad. They may quarantine at any time."

"Dr. Pruyn ought to be here any day now. Let's leave that matter for him. There's a man I have confidence in."

"Mr. Perkins says that Dr. Pruyn will bottle up the port tighter than the Dutch."

"Let him, so long as we get out first. Now, Polly, you tell this man Perkins that I'll pay all expenses and give him a round hundred for himself if he'll bring me a receipt showing that my cablegram has been dispatched to Washington."

"I don't think I'd quite like to do that, dad. He isn't the sort of man one offers money to."

"Every one's the sort of man one offers money to - if it's enough," retorted her father. "And a hundred dollars will look pretty big to a scientific man. I know something about their salaries. You try him."

"So far as expenses go, I will. But I won't hurt his feelings by trying to pay him for something that he would do for friendship or not at all."

"Have it your own way. When is he coming in?"

"He isn't coming in."

"Then where are you going to see him?"

"Up on the mountain trail, when I ride tomorrow afternoon."

"With Carroll?"

"No; I'm going alone."

"I don't quite like to have you knocking about mountain roads by yourself, though Mr. Sherwen says you're safe anywhere here. Where's that little automatic revolver I gave you?"

"In my trunk. I'll carry that if it will make you feel any easier."

"Yes, do. But I can't see why you can't send word to Perkins that I want to see him here."

"I can. And I can guess just what his answer would be."

"Well, guess ahead."

"He'd tell you to go to the bad place, or its scientific equivalent." She laughed.

"Would he?" Mr. Brewster did not laugh. "And perhaps you'll be good enough to tell me why."

"Because you sent word that you were out when he called."

"Humph! I see people when *I* want to see THEM, not when they want to see me."

"Then Mr. Perkins is likely to prove permanently invisible to you, if I'm any judge of character."

"Well, well," said Mr. Brewster impatiently, "manage it yourself. Only impress on him the necessity of getting the message on the wire. I'll write it out to-night and give it to you with the money to-morrow."

After luncheon on the following day, Polly, with the cablegram and money in her purse and her automatic safely disposed in her belt, walked in the plaza with Carroll. The legless beggar whined at them for alms. Handing him a quartillo, the Southerner would have passed on, but his companion stood eyeing the mendicant.

"Now, what can there be in that poor wreck to captivate the scientific intellect?" she marveled.

"If you mean Mr. Perkins - " began Carroll.

"I do."

"Then I think perhaps the reason for some of that gentleman's associations will hardly stand inquiry."

The girl turned her eyes on him and searched the handsome, serious face.

"Fitz, you're not the man to say that of another man without some good reason."

"I am not, Miss Polly."

"You think that Mr. Perkins is not the kind of man for me to have anything to do with?"

"I - I'm afraid he isn't."

"Don't you think that, having gone so far, you ought to tell me why?"

Carroll flushed.

"I would rather tell your father."

"Are you implying a scandal in connection with my timid, little dried-up scientist?"

"I'm only saying," said the other doggedly, "that there's something secret and underhanded about that place of his in the mountains. It's a matter of common gossip."

The girl laughed outright.

"The poor beetle man! Why, he's so afraid of a woman that he goes all to pieces if one speaks to him suddenly. Just to see his expression, I'd like to tell him that he's being scandalized by all Caracuna."

"You're going to see him again?"

"Certainly. This afternoon."

"I don't think you should, Miss Polly."

"Have you any actual facts against him? Anything but casual gossip?"

"No; not yet."

"When you have, I'll listen to you. But you couldn't make me believe it, anyway. Why, Fitz, look at him!"

"Take me with you," insisted the other, "and let me ask him a question or two that any honorable man could answer. They don't call him the Unspeakable Perk for nothing, Miss Polly."

"It's just because they don't understand his type. Nor do you, Fitz, and so you mistrust him."

"I understand that you've shown more interest in him than in any one you know," said the other miserably.

Her laugh rang as free and frank as a child's.

"Interest? That's true. But if you mean sentiment, Fitz, after once having looked into the depths of those absurd goggles, can you, COULD you think of sentiment and the beetle man in the same breath?"

"No, I couldn't," he confessed, relieved. "But, then, I never have been able to understand you, Miss Polly."

"Therein lies my fatal charm," she said saucily. "Now, to the beetle man, I'm a specimen. HE understands as much as he wants to. Probably I shall never see him after to-day, anyway. He's going to get a message through for us that will deliver us from this land of bondage."

"He can't do it - too soon for me," declared Carroll. "And, Miss Polly, you don't think the worse of me for having said behind his back what I'm just waiting to say to his face?"

"Not a bit," said the girl warmly. "Only I know it's nonsense."

"I hope so," said Carroll, quite honestly. "I would hate to think anything low-down of a man you'd call your friend."

Carroll had learned more than he had told, but less than enough to give him what he considered proper evidence to lay before Polly's father. After some deliberation as to the point of honor involved, he decided to go to Raimonda, who, alone in Caracuna City, seemed to be on personal terms with the hermit. He found the young man in his office. With entire frankness, Carroll stated his errand and the reason for it. The Caracunan heard him with grave courtesy.

"And now, senior," concluded the American, "here's my question, and it's for you to determine whether, under the circumstances, you are justified in giving me an answer. Is there a woman living in Mr. Perkins's quinta on the mountains?"

"I cannot answer that question," said the other, after some deliberation.

"I'm sorry," said Carroll simply.

"I also. The more so in that my attitude may be misconstrued against Mr. Perkins. I am bound by confidence."

"So I infer," returned his visitor courteously. "Then I have only to ask your pardon - "

"One moment, if you please, senor. Perhaps this will serve to make easy your mind. On my word, there is nothing in Mr. Perkins's life on the mountain in any manner dishonorable or - or irregular."

In a flash, the simple solution crossed Carroll's mind. That a woman was there, and a woman not of the servant class, could hardly be doubted, in view of almost direct evidence from eyewitnesses. If there was nothing irregular about her presence, it was because she was Perkins's wife. In view of Raimonda's attitude, he did not feel free to put the direct query. Another question would serve his purpose.

"Is it advisable, and for the best interests of Miss Brewster, that she should associate with him under the circumstances?"

The Caracunan started and shot a glance at his interlocutor that said, as plainly as words, "How much do you know that you are not telling?" had the latter not been too intent upon his own theory to interpret it.

"Ah, that," said Raimonda, after a pause, - "that is another question. If it were my sister, or any one dear to me - but" - he shrugged - "views on that matter differ."

"I hardly think that yours and mine differ, senior. I thank you for bearing with me with so much patience."

He went out with his suspicions hardened into certainty.

VII

THAT WHICH THY SERVANT IS

A man that you'd call your friend. Such had been Fitzhugh Carroll's reference to the Unspeakable Perk. With that characterization in her mind, Miss Brewster let herself drift, after her suitor had left her, into a dreamy consideration of the hermit's attitude toward her. She was not prone lightly to employ the terms of friendship, yet this new and casual acquaintance had shown a readiness to serve - not as cavalier, but as friend - none too common in the experience of the much-courted and a little spoiled beauty. Being, indeed, a "lady nowise bitter to those who served her with good intent," she reflected, with a kindly light in her eyes, that it was all part and parcel of the beetle's man's amiable queerness.

Still musing upon this queerness, she strolled back to find her mount waiting at the corner of the plaza. In consideration of the heat she let her cream-colored mule choose his own pace, so they proceeded quite slowly up the hill road, both absorbed in meditation, which ceased only when the mule started an argument about a turn in the trail. He was a well-bred trotting mule, worth six hundred dollars in gold of any man's money, and he was self-appreciative in knowledge of the fact. He brought a singular firmness of purpose to

Samuel Hopkins Adams

the support of the negative of her proposition, which was that he should swing north from the broad into the narrow path. When the debate was over, St. John the Baptist - this, I hesitate to state, yet must, it being the truth, was the spirited animal's name - was considerably chastened, and Miss Brewster more than a trifle flushed. She left him tied to a ceiba branch at the exit from the dried creek bed, with strict instructions not to kick, lest a worse thing befall him. Miss Brewster's fighting blood was up, when, ten minutes late, because of the episode, she reached the summit of the rock.

"Oh, Mr. Beetle Man, are you there?" she called.

"Yes, Voice. You sound strange. What is it?"

"I've been hurrying, and if you tell me I'm late, I'll - I'll fall on your neck again and break it."

"Has anything happened?"

"Nothing in particular. I've been boxing the compass with a mule. It's tiresome."

He reflected.

"You're not, by any chance, speaking figuratively of your respected parent?"

"Certainly NOT!" she disclaimed indignantly. "This was a real mule. You're very impertinent."

"Well, you see, he was impertinent to me, saying he was out when he was in. What is his decision - yes or no?"

"No."

A sharp exclamation came from the nook below.

"Is that the entomological synonym for 'damn'?" she inquired.

"It's a lament for time wasted on a - Well, never mind that."

"But he wants you to carry a message by that secret route of yours. Will you do it for him?"

"NO!"

"That's not being a very kind or courteous beetle man."

"I owe Mr. Brewster no courtesy."

"And you pay only where you owe? Just, but hardly amiable. Well, you owe me nothing - but - will you do it for me?"

"Yes."

"Without even knowing what it is?"

"Yes."

"In return you shall have your heart's desire."

"Doubted."

"Isn't the dearest wish of your soul to drive me out of Caracuna?"

"Hum! Well - er - yes. Yes; of course it is."

"Very well. If you can get dad's message on the wire to Washington, he thinks the Secretary of State, who is his friend, can reach the Dutch and have them open up the blockade for us."

"Time apparently meaning nothing to him."

"Would it take much time?"

"About four days to a wire."

She gazed at him in amazement.

"And you were willing to give up four days to carry my message through, 'unsight - unseen,' as we children used to say?"

"Willing enough, but not able to. I'd have got a messenger through with it, if necessary. But in four days, there'll be other obstacles besides the Dutch."

"Quarantine?"

"Yes."

"I thought that had to wait for Dr. Pruyn."

"Pruyn's here. That's a secret, Miss Brewster."

"Do you know EVERYTHING? Has he found plague?"

"Ah, I don't say that. But he will find it, for it's certainly here. I satisfied myself of that yesterday."

"From your beggar friend?"

"What made you think that, O most acute observer?"

"What else would you be talking to him of, with such interest?"

"You're correct. Bubonic always starts in the poor quarters. To know how people die, you have to know how they live. So I cultivated my beggar friend and listened to the gossip of quick funerals and unexplained disappearances. I'd have had some real arguments to present to Mr. Brewster if he had cared to listen."

"He'll listen to Dr. Pruyn. They're old friends."

"No! Are they?"

"Yes. Since college days. So perhaps the quarantine will be easier to get through than the blockade."

"Do you think so? I'm afraid you'll find that pull doesn't work with the service that Dr. Pruyn is in."

"And you think that there will be quarantine within four days?"

"Almost sure to be."

"Then, of course, I needn't trouble you with the message."

"Don't jump at conclusions. There might be another and quicker way."

"Wireless?" she asked quickly.

"No wireless on the island. No. This way you'll just have to trust me for."

"I'll trust you for anything you say you can do."

"But I don't say I can. I say only that I'll try."

"That's enough for me. Ready! Now, brace yourself. I'm coming down."

"Wh - why - wait! Can't you send it down?"

"No. Besides, you KNOW you want to see me. No use pretending, after last time. Remember your verse now, and I'll come slowly."

Solemnly he began: -

> *"Scarab, tarantula, neurop - "*
> *"'Doodle-bug,'" she prompted severely.*
> *" - doodle-bug, flea," -*

he concluded obediently.

> *"Scarab, tarantula, doodle-bug, flea.*
> *Scarab, tarantula, doodle - "*

"Oof! I - I - didn't think you'd be here so soon!"

He scrambled to his feet, hardly less palpitating than on the occasion of their first encounter.

"Hopeless!" she mourned. "Incurable! Wanted: a miracle of St. Vitus. Do stop nibbling your hat, and sit down."

"I don't think it's as bad as it was," he murmured, obeying. "One gets accustomed to you."

"One gets accustomed to anything in time, even the eccentricities of one's friends."

"Do you think I'm eccentric?"

"Do I think - Have you ever known any one who didn't think you eccentric?"

Upon this he pondered solemnly.

"It's so long since I've stopped to consider what people think of me. One hasn't time, you know."

"Then one is unhuman. *I* have time."

"Of course. But you haven't anything else to do."

As this was quite true, she naturally felt annoyed.

"Knowing as you do all the secrets of my inner life," she observed sarcastically, "of course you are in a position to judge."

Her own words recalled Carroll's charge, and though, with the subject of them before her, it seemed ridiculously impossible, yet the spirit of mischief, ever hovering about her like an attendant sprite, descended and took possession of her speech. She assumed a severely judicial expression.

"Mr. Beetle Man, will you lay your hand upon your microscope, or whatever else scientists make oath upon, and answer fully and truly the question about to be put to you?"

"As I hope for a blessed release from this abode of lunacy, I will."

"Mr. Beetle Man, have you got an awful secret in your life?"

So sharply did he start that the heavy goggles slipped a fraction of an inch along his nose, the first time she had ever seen them in any degree misplaced. She was herself sensibly discountenanced by his perturbation.

"Why do you ask that?" he demanded.

"Natural interest in a friend," she answered lightly, but with growing wonder. "I think you'd be altogether irresistible if you were a pirate or a smuggler or a revolutionary. The romantic spirit could lurk so securely behind those gloomy soul-screens that you wear. What do you keep back of them, O dark and shrouded beetle man?"

"My eyes," he grunted.

"Basilisk eyes, I'm sure. And what behind the eyes?"

"My thoughts."

"You certainly keep them securely. No intruders allowed. But you haven't answered my question. Have you ever murdered any one in cold blood? Or are you a married man trifling with the affections of poor little me?"

"You shall know all," he began, in the leisurely tone of

one who commences a long narrative. "My parents were honest, but poor. At the age of three years and four months, a maternal uncle, who, having been a proofreader of Abyssinian dialect stories for a ladies' magazine, was considered a literary prophet, foretold that I -"

"Help! Wait! Stop! -

> *"'Oh, skip your dear uncle!' the bellman exclaimed,*
> *And impatiently tinkled his bell."*

Her companion promptly capped her verse: -

> *"'I skip forty years,' said the baker in tears,"* -

"You can't," she objected. "If you skipped half that, I don't believe it would leave you much."

"When one is giving one's life history by request," he began, with dignity, "interruptions - "

"It isn't by request," she protested. "I don't want your life history. I won't have it! You shan't treat an unprotected and helpless stranger so. Besides, I'm much more interested to know how you came to be familiar with Lewis Carroll."

"Just because I've wasted my career on frivolous trifles like science, you needn't think I've wholly neglected the true inwardness of life, as exemplified in 'The Hunting of the Snark,'" he said gravely.

"Do you know" - she leaned forward, searching his face - "I believe you came out of that book yourself. ARE you a Boojum? Will you, unless I 'charm you with smiles and soap,'

> *"'Softly and silently vanish away,*
> *And never be heard of again'?"*

"You're mixed. YOU'D be the one to do that if I were a real Boojum. And you'll be doing it soon enough, anyway," he concluded ruefully.

"So I shall, but don't be too sure that I'll 'never be heard of again.'"

He glanced up at the sun, which was edging behind a dark cloud, over the gap.

"Is your raging thirst for personal information sufficiently slaked?" he asked. "We've still fifteen or twenty minutes left."

"Is that all? And I haven't yet given you the message!" She drew it from the bag and handed it to him.

"Sealed," he observed.

The girl colored painfully.

"Dad didn't intend - You mustn't think - " With a flash of generous wrath she tore the envelope open and held out the inclosure. "But I shouldn't have thought you so concerned with formalities," she commented curiously.

"It isn't that. But in some respects, possibly important, it would be better if - " He stopped, looking at her doubtfully.

"Read it," she nodded.

He ran through the brief document.

"Yes; it's just as well that I should know. I'll leave a copy."

Something in his accent made her scrutinize him.

"You're going into danger!" she cried.

"Danger? No; I think not. Difficulty, perhaps. But I think it can be put through."

"If it were dangerous, you'd do it just the same," she said, almost accusingly.

"It would be worth some danger now to get you away from greater danger later. See here, Miss Brewster" - he rose and stood over her - "there must be no mistake or misunderstanding about this."

"Don't gloom at me with those awful glasses," she said fretfully. "I feel as if I were being stared at by a hidden person."

He disregarded the protest.

"If I get this message through, can you guarantee that your father will take out the yacht as soon as the Dutch send word to him?"

"Oh, yes. He will do that. How are you going to deliver the message?"

Again her words might as well not have been spoken.

" You'd better have your luggage ready for a

quick start."

"Will it be soon?"

"It may be."

"How shall we know?"

"I will get word to you."

"Bring it?"

He shook his head.

"No; I fear not. This is good-bye."

"You're very casual about it," she said, aggrieved. "At least, it would be polite to pretend."

"What am I to pretend?"

"To be sorry. Aren't you sorry? Just a little bit?"

"Yes; I'm sorry. Just a little bit - at least."

"I'm most awfully sorry myself," she said frankly. "I shall miss you."

"As a curiosity?" he asked, smiling.

"As a friend. You have been a friend to us - to me," she amended sweetly. "Each time I see you, I have more the feeling that you've been more of a friend than I know."

"'That which thy servant is,'" he quoted lightly. But

beneath the lightness she divined a pain that she could not wholly fathom. Quite aware of her power, Miss Polly Brewster was now, for one of the few times in her life, stricken with contrition for her use of it.

"And I - I haven't been very nice," she faltered. "I'm afraid" sometimes I've been quite horrid."

"You? You've been 'the glory and the dream.' I shall be needing memories for a while. And when the glory has gone, at least the dream will remain - tethered."

"But I'm not going to be a dream alone," she said, with wistful lightness. "It's far too much like being a ghost. I'm going to be a friend, if you'll let me. And I'm going to write to you, if you will tell me where. You won't find it so very easy to make a mere memory of me. And when you come home - When ARE you coming home?"

He shook his head.

"Then you must find out, and let me know. And you must come and visit us at our summer place, where there's a mountain-side that we can sit on, and you can pretend that our lake is the Caribbean and hate it to your heart's content -"

"I don't believe I can ever quite hate the Caribbean again."

"From this view you mustn't, anyway. I shouldn't like that. As for our lake, nobody could really help loving it. So you must be sure and come, won't you?"

"Dreams!" he murmured.

"Isn't there room in the scientific life for dreams?"

"Yes. But not for their fulfillment."

"But there will be beetles and dragon-flies on our mountain," she went on, conscious of talking against time, of striving to put off the moment of departure. "You'll find plenty of work there. Do you know, Mr. Beetle Man, you haven't told me a thing, really, about your work, or a thing, really, about yourself. Is that the way to treat a friend?"

"When I undertook to spread before you the true and veracious history of my life," he began, striving to make his tone light, "you would none of it."

"Are you determined to put me off? Do you think that I wouldn't find the things that are real to you interesting?"

"They're quite technical," he said shyly.

"But they are the big things to you, aren't they? They make life for you?"

"Oh, yes; that, of course." It was as if he were surprised at the need of such a question. "I suppose I find the same excitement and adventure in research that other men find in politics, or war, or making money."

"Adventure?" she said, puzzled. "I shouldn't have supposed research an adventurous career, exactly."

"No; not from the outside." His hidden gaze shifted to sweep the far distances. His voice dropped and softened, and, when he spoke again, she felt vaguely and strangely that he was hardly thinking of her or her question, except as a part of the great wonder-world surrounding and enfolding their companioned remoteness.

"This is my credo," he said, and quoted, half under his breath: -

> *"'We have come in search of truth,*
> *Trying with uncertain key*
> *Door by door of mystery.*
> *We are reaching, through His laws,*
> *To the garment hem of Cause.*
> *As, with fingers of the blind,*
> *We are groping here to find*
> *What the hieroglyphics mean*
> *Of the Unseen in the seen;*
> *What the Thought which underlies*
> *Nature's masking and disguise;*
> *What it is that hides beneath*
> *Blight and bloom and birth and death.'"*

Other men had poured poetry into Polly Brewster's ears, and she had thought them vapid or priggish or affected, according as they had chosen this or that medium. This man was different. For all his outer grotesquery, the noble simplicity of the verse matched some veiled and hitherto but half-expressed quality within him, and dignified him. Miss Brewster suffered the strange but not wholly unpleasant sensation of feeling herself dwindle.

"It's very beautiful," she said, with an effort. "Is it Matthew Arnold?"

"Nearer home. You an American, and don't know your Whittier? That passage from his 'Agassiz' comes pretty near to being what life means to me. Have I answered your requirements?"

"Fully and finely."

She rose from the rock upon which she had been seated, and stretched out both hands to him. He took and held them without awkwardness or embarrassment. By that alone she could have known that he was suffering with a pain that submerged consciousness of self.

"Whether I see you again or not, I'll never forget you," she said softly. "You HAVE been good to me, Mr. Perkins."

"I like the other name better," he said.

"Of course. Mr. Beetle Man." She laughed a little tremulously. Abruptly she stamped a determined foot. "I'm NOT going away without having seen my friend for once. Take off your glasses, Mr. Beetle Man."

"Too much radiance is bad for the microscopical eye."

"The sun is under a cloud."

"But you're here, and you'd glow in the dark."

"No; I'm not to be put off with pretty speeches. Take them off. Please!"

Releasing her hand, he lifted off the heavy and disfiguring apparatus, and stood before her, quietly submissive to her wish. She took a quick step backward, stumbled, and thrust out a hand against the face of the giant rock for support.

"Oh!" she cried, and again, "Oh, I didn't think you'd look like that!"

"What is it? Is there anything very wrong with me?" he asked seriously, blinking a little in the soft light.

"No, no. It isn't that. I - I hardly know - I expected something different. Forgive me for being so - so stupid."

In truth, Miss Polly Brewster had sustained a shock. She had become accustomed to regard her beetle man rather more in the light of a beetle than a man. In fact, the human side of him had impressed her only as a certain dim appeal to sympathy; the masculine side had simply not existed. Now it was as if he had unmasked. The visage, so grotesque and gnomish behind its mechanical apparatus, had given place to a wholly different and formidably strange face. The change all centered in the eyes. They were wide-set eyes of the clearest, steadiest, and darkest gray she had ever met; and they looked out at her from sharply angled brows with a singular clarity and calmness of regard. In their light the man's face became instinct with character in every line. Strength was there, self-control, dignity, a glint of humor in the little wrinkles at the corner of the mouth, and, withal a sort of quiet and sturdy beauty.

She had half-turned her face from him. Now, as her gaze returned and was fixed by his, she felt a wave of blood expand her heart, rush upward into her cheeks, and press into her eyes tears of swift regret. But now she was sorry, not for him, but for herself, because he had become remote and difficult to her.

"Have I startled you?" he asked curiously. "I'll put them back on again."

"No, no; don't do that!" She rallied herself to the point of laughing a little. "I'm a goose. You see, I've pictured you as quite different. Have you ever seen yourself in the glass with those dreadful disguises on?"

"Why, no; I don't suppose I have," he replied, after reflection. "After all, they're meant for use, not for ornament."

By this time she had mastered her confusion and was able to examine his face. Under his eyes were circles of dull gray, defined by deep lines,

"Why, you're worn out!" she cried pitifully. "Haven't you been sleeping?"

"Not much."

"You must take something for it." The mothering instinct sprang to the rescue. "How much rest did you get last night?"

"Let me see. Last night I did very well. Fully four hours."

"And that is more than you average?"

"Well, yes; lately. You see, I've been pretty busy."

"Yet you've given up your time to my wretched,

unimportant little stupid affairs! And what return have I made?"

"You've made the sun shine," he said, "in a rather shaded existence."

"Promise me that you'll sleep to-night; that you won't work a stroke."

"No; I can't promise that."

"You'll break down. You'll go to pieces. What have you got to do more important than keeping in condition?"

"As to that, I'll last through. And there's some business that won't wait."

Divination came upon her.

"Dad's message!"

"If it weren't that, it would be something else."

Her hand went out to him, and was withdrawn.

"Please put on your glasses," she said shyly.

Smiling, he did her bidding.

"There! Now you are my beetle man again. No, not quite, though. You'll never be quite the same beetle man again."

"I shall always be," he contradicted gently.

"Anyway, it's better. You're easier to say things to. Are you really the man who ran away from the street car?" she asked doubtfully.

"I really am."

"Then I'm most surely sure that you had good reason." She began to laugh softly. "As for the stories about you, I'd believe them less than ever, now."

"Are there stories about me?"

"Gossip of the club. They call you 'The Unspeakable Perk'!"

"Not a bad nickname," he admitted. "I expect I have been rather unspeakable, from their point of view."

A desire to have the faith that was in her supported by this man's own word overrode her shyness.

"Mr. Beetle Man," she said, "have you got a sister?"

"I? No. Why?"

"If you had a sister, is there anything - Oh, DARN your sister!" broke forth the irrepressible Polly. "I'll be your sister for this. Is there anything about you and your life here that you'd be afraid to tell me?"

"No."

"I knew there wasn't," she said contentedly. She hesitated a moment, then put a hand on his arm. "Does this HAVE to be good-bye, Mr. Beetle Man?" she said wistfully.

"I'm afraid so."

"No!" She stamped imperiously. "I want to see you again, and I'm going to see you again. Won't you come down to the port and bring me another bunch of your mountain orchids when we sail - just for good-bye?"

Through the dull medium of the glasses she could feel his eyes questioning hers. And she knew that once more before she sailed away, she must look into those eyes, in all their clarity and all their strength - and then try to forget them. The swift color ran up into her cheeks.

"I - I suppose so," he said. "Yes."

"Au revoir, then!" she cried, with a thrill of gladness, and fled up the rock.

The Unspeakable Perk strode down his path, broke into a trot, and held to it until he reached his house. But Miss Polly, departing in her own direction, stopped dead after ten minutes' going. It had struck her forcefully that she had forgotten the matter of the expense of the message. How could she reach him? She remembered the cliff above the rock, and the signal. If a signal was valid in one direction, it ought to work equally well in the other. She had her automatic with her. Retracing her steps, she ascended the cliff, a rugged climb. Across the deep-fringed chasm she could plainly see the porch of the quinta with the little clearing at the side, dim in the clouded light. Drawing the revolver, she fired three shots.

"He'll come," she thought contentedly.

The sun broke from behind the obscuring cloud and sent a shaft of light straight down upon the clearing. It illumined with pitiless distinctness the shimmering silk of a woman's dress, hanging on a line and waving in the first draft of the evening breeze. For a moment Polly stood transfixed. What did it mean? Was it perhaps a servant's dress. No; he had told her that there was no woman servant.

As she sought the solution, a woman's figure emerged from the porch of the quinta, crossed the compound, and dropped upon a bench. Even at that distance, the watcher could tell from the woman's bearing and apparel that she was not of the servant class. She seemed to be gazing out over the mountains; there was something dreary and forlorn in her attitude. What, then, did she do in the beetle man's house?

Below the rock the shrubbery weaved and thrashed, and the person who could best answer that question burst into view at a full lope.

"What is it?" he panted. "Was it you who fired?"

She stared at him mutely. The revolver hung in her hand. In a moment he was beside her.

"Has anything happened?" he began again, then turned his head to follow the direction of her regard. He saw the figure in the compound.

"Good God in heaven!" he groaned.

He caught the revolver from her hand and fired three slow shots. The woman turned. Snatching off his hat, he signalled violently with it. The woman rose and, as it seemed to Polly Brewster, moved in humble submissiveness back to the shelter.

White consternation was stamped on the Unspeakable Perk's face as he handed the revolver to its owner.

"Do you need me?" he asked quickly. "If not, I must go back at once."

"I do not need you," said the girl, in level tones. "You lied to me."

His expression changed. She read in it the desperation of guilt.

"I can explain," he said hurriedly, "but not now. There isn't time. Wait here. I'll be back. I'll be back the instant I can get away."

As he spoke, he was halfway down the rock, headed for the lower trail. The bushes closed behind him.

Painfully Polly Brewster made her way down the treacherous footing of the cliff path to her place on the rock. From her bag she drew one of her cards, wrote slowly and carefully a few words, found a dry stick, set it between two rocks, and pinned her message to it. Then she ran, as helpless humans run from the scourge of their own hearts.

Half an hour later the hermit, sweat-covered and breathless, returned to the rock. For a moment he gazed about, bewildered by the silence. The white card caught his eye. He read its angular scrawl.

"I wish never to see you again. Never! Never! Never!"

A sulphur-yellow inquisitor, of a more insinuating manner than the former participant in their conversation, who had been examining the message on his own account, flew to the top of the cliff.

"Qu'est-ce qu'elle dit? Qu'est-ce qu'elle dit?" he demanded.

For the first time in his adult life the beetle man threw a stone at a bird.

VIII

LOS YANKIS

Luncheon on the day following the kiskadee bird's narrow squeak for his life was a dreary affair for Mr. Fitzhugh Carroll. Business had called Mr. Brewster away. This deprivation the Southerner would have borne with equanimity. But Miss Brewster had also absented herself, which was rather too much for the devoted, but apprehensive, lover. Thus, ample time was given him to consider how ill his suit was prospering. The longer he stayed, the less he saw of Miss Polly. That she was kinder and more gentle, less given to teasing him than of yore, was poor compensation. He was shrewd enough to draw no good augury from that. Something had altered her, and he was divided between suspicion of the last week's mail, the arrival of which had been about contemporaneous with her change of spirit, and some local cause. Was a letter from Smith, the millionaire, or Bobby, the friend of her childhood, responsible? Or was the cause nearer at hand?

For one preposterous moment he thought of the Unspeakable Perk. A quick visualization of that gnomish, froggish face was enough to dispel the suspicion. At least the petted and rather fastidious Miss Brewster's fancy would be captured only by a gentleman, not by any such homunculus as the mountain dweller. Her interest, perhaps; the man possessed the bizarre attraction of the freakish. But anything else was absurd. And the knight was inclined to attaint his lady for a certain cruelty in the matter; she was being something less than fair to the Unspeakable Perk.

The searchlight of his surmise ranged farther. Raimonda! The young Caracunan was handsome, distinguished, manly, with a romantic charm that the American did not underestimate. He, at least, was a gentleman, and the assiduity of his attentions to the Northern beauty had become the joke of the clubs - except when Raimonda was present. By the same token, half of the gilded youth of the capital, and most of the young diplomats, were the sworn slaves of the girl. It was a confused field, indeed. Well, thank Heaven, she would soon be out of it! Word had come down from her that she was busy packing her things. Carroll wandered about the hotel, waiting for the news that would explain this preparation.

It came, at mid-afternoon, in the person of Miss Polly herself. Why packing trunks, with the aid of an experienced maid, should, even in a hot climate, produce heavy circles under the eyes, a droop at the mouth corners, and a complete submersion of vivacity, is a problem which Carroil then and there gave up. He had too much tact to question or comment.

"Oh, I'm so tired!" she said, giving him her hand. "Have you much packing to do, Fitzhugh?"

"No one has given me any notice to get ready, Miss Polly."

"How very neglectful of me! We may leave at any time."

"Yes; you may. But my ship doesn't seem to be coming in very fast."

The double entente was unintentional, but the girl winced.

"Aren't you coming with us on the yacht?"

"Am I?" His handsome face lighted hopefully.

"Of course. Dad expects you to. What kind of people should we be to leave any friend behind, with matters as they are?"

"Ah, yes." The hope passed out of his face. "Dictates of humanity, and that sort of thing. I think, if you and Mr. Brewster -"

"Please don't be silly, Fitz," she pleaded. "You know it would make me most unhappy to leave you."

Rarely did the scion of Southern blood and breeding lose the self-control and reserve on which he prided himself, but he had been harassed by events to an unwonted strain of temper.

"Is it making you unhappy to leave any one else here?" he blurted out.

The challenge stirred the girl's spirit.

"No, indeed! I wouldn't care if I never saw any of them again. I'm tired of it all. I want to go home," she said, like a pathetic child.

"Oh, Miss Polly," he began, taking a step toward her, "if you'd only let me -"

She put up one little sunburned hand.

"Please, Fitz! I - I don't feel up to it to-day."

Humbly he subsided.

"I'd no right to ask you the question," he apologized. "It was kind of you to answer me at all."

"You're really a dear, Fitz," she said, smiling a little wanly. "Sometimes I wish -"

She did not finish her sentence, but wandered over to the window, and gazed out across the square. On the far side something quite out of the ordinary seemed to be going on.

"The legless beggar seems to have collected quite an audience," she remarked idly.

Her suitor joined her on the parlor balcony.

"Possibly he's starting a revolution. Any one can do it down here."

Vehement adjuration, in a high, strident voice, came floating across to them.

"Listen!" cried the girl. "He's speaking. English, isn't he?"

"It seems to be a mixture of English, French, and Spanish. Quite a polyglot the friend of your friend Perkins appears to be."

She turned steady eyes upon him.

"Mr. Perkins is not my friend."

"No?"

"I never want to see him, or to hear his name again."

"Ah, then you've found out about him?"

"Yes." She flushed. "Yes - at least - Yes," she concluded.

"He admitted it to you?"

"No, he lied about it."

"I think I shall go up and make a call on Mr. Perkins," said Carroll, with formidable quiet.

"Oh, it doesn't matter," she answered wearily. "He'd only run away and hide." As she said it, her inner self convicted her tongue of lying.

"Very likely. Yet, see here, Miss Polly, - I want to be fair to that fellow. It doesn't follow that because he's a coward he's a cad."

"He isn't a coward!" she flashed.

"You just said yourself that he'd run and hide."

"Well, he wouldn't, and he IS a cad."

"As you like. In any case, I shall make it a point to see him before I leave. If he can explain, well and good. If not - " He did not conclude.

"Our orator seems to have finished," observed the girl. "I shall go back upstairs and write some good-bye notes to the kind people here."

"Just for curiosity, I think I'll drive across and look at the legless Demosthenes," said her companion. "I was going to do a little shopping, anyway. So I'll report later, if he's revoluting or anything exciting."

From her own balcony, when she reached it, Polly had a less obstructed view of the beggar's appropriated corner, and she looked out a few minutes after she reached the room to see whether he had resumed his oratory. Apparently he had not, for the crowd had melted away. The legless one was rocking himself monotonously upon his stumps. His head was sunk forward, and from his extraordinary mouthings the spectator judged that he must be talking to himself with resumed vehemence. From what next passed before her astonished vision, Miss Brewster would have suspected herself of a hallucination of delirium had she not been sure of normal health.

One of the well-horsed, elegant little public victorias with which the city is so well supplied stopped at the curb, and the handsome head of Preston Fairfax Fitzhugh Carroll was thrust forth. At almost the same moment the Unspeakable Perk appeared upon the steps. He was wearing a pair of enormous, misfit white gloves. He went down to the beggar, reached forth a hand, and, to the far-away spectator's wonder-struck interpretation, seemed to thrust something, presumably a document, into the breast of the mendicant's shirt. Having performed this strange rite, he leaped up the steps, hesitated, rushed over to Carroll's equipage, and laid violent hands upon the occupant, with obvious intent to draw him forth. For a moment they seemed to struggle upon the sidewalk; then both rushed upon the unfortunate beggar and proceeded to kidnap him and thrust him bodily into the cab.

The driver turned in his seat at this point, his cue in the mad farce having been given, and opened speech with many gestures, whereupon Carroll arose and embraced him warmly. And with this grouping, the vehicle, bearing its lunatic load, sped around the corner and disappeared, while the sole interested witness retired to obscurity, with her reeling head between her hands.

One final touch of phantasy was given to the whole affair when, two hours later, she met Carroll, soiled and grimy, coming across the plaza, smoking - he, the addict to thirty-cent Havanas! - an awful native cheroot, whose incense spread desolation about him. Further and more extraordinary, when she essayed to obtain a solution of the mystery from him, he repelled her with emphatic gestures and a few half-strangled words with whose unintelligibility the cheroot fumes may have had some connection, and hurried into the hotel, where he remained in seclusion the rest of the day.

What in the name of all the wonders could it mean? On Mr. Brewster's return, she laid the matter before him at the dinner table.

"Touch of the sun, perhaps," he hazarded. "Nothing else I know of would explain it."

"Do two Americans, a half-breed beggar, and a local coachman get sunstruck at one and the same time?" she inquired disdainfully.

"Doesn't seem likely. By your account, though, the crippled beggar seems to have been the little Charlie Ross of melodrama."

"Then why didn't he shout for help? I listened, but didn't hear a sound from him."

"Movie-picture rehearsal," grunted Mr. Brewster. "I can't quite see the heir of all the Virginias in the part. Isn't he coming down to dinner this evening?"

"His dinner was sent up to his room. Isn't it extraordinary?"

"Ask Sherwen about it. He's coming around this evening for coffee in our rooms."

But the American representative had something else on his mind besides casual kidnapings.

"I've just come from a talk with the British Minister," he remarked, setting down his cup. "He's officially in charge of American interests, you know."

"Thought you were," said Mr. Brewster.

"Officially, I have no existence. The United States of America is wiped off the map, so far as the sovereign Republic of Caracuna is concerned. Some of its politicians wouldn't be over-grieved if the local Americans underwent the same process. The British Minister would, I'm sure, sleep easier if you were all a thousand miles away from here."

"Tell Sir Willet that he's very ungallant," pouted Miss Polly. "When I sat next to him at dinner last week he offered to establish woman suffrage here and elect me next president if I'd stay."

Sherwen hardly paid this the tribute of a smile.

"That was before he found out certain things. The Hochwald Legation" - he lowered his voice - "is undoubtedly stirring up anti- American sentiment."

"But why?" inquired Mr. Brewster. "There's enough trade for them and for us?"

"For one thing, they don't like your concessions, Mr. Brewster. Then they have heard that Dr. Pruyn is on his way, and they want to make all the trouble they can for him, and make it impossible for him to get actual information of the presence of plague. I happen to know that their consul is officially declaring fake all the plague rumors."

"That suits me," declared the magnate. "We don't want to have to run Dutch and quarantine blockade both."

"Meantime, there are two or three cheap but dangerous demagogues who have been making anti-'Yanki,' as they call us, speeches in the slums. Sir Willet doesn't like the looks of it. If there were any way in which you could get through, and to sea, it would be well to take it at once. Am I correct in supposing that you've taken steps to clear the yacht, Mr. Brewster?"

"Yes. That is, I've sent a message. Or, at least, so my daughter, to whose management I left it, believes."

"Don't tell me how," said Sherwen quickly. "There is reason to believe that it has been dispatched."

"You've heard something?"

"I have a message from our consul at Puerto del Norte, Mr. Wisner."

"For me?" asked the concessionaire.

"Why, no," was the hesitant reply. "It isn't quite clear, but it seems to be for Miss Brewster."

"Why not?" inquired that young lady coolly. "What is it?"

"The best I could make of it over the phone - Wisner had to be guarded - was that people planning to take Dutch leave would better pay their parting calls by to-morrow at the latest."

"That would mean day after to-morrow, wouldn't it?" mused the girl.

"If it means anything at all," substituted her father testily.

"Meantime, how do you like the Gran Hotel Kast, Miss Brewster?" asked Sherwen.

"It's awful beyond words! I've done nothing but wish

for a brigade of Biddies, with good stout mops, and a government permit to clean up. I'd give it a bath!"

"Yes, it's pretty bad. I'm glad you don't like it."

"Glad? Is every one ag'in' poor me?"

"Because - well, the American Legation is a very lonely place. Now, the presence of an American lady -"

"Are you offering a proposal of marriage, Mr. Sherwen?" twinkled the girl. "If so - Dad, please leave the room."

"Knock twenty years off my battle-scarred life and you wouldn't be safe a minute," he retorted. "But, no. This is a measure of safety. Sir Willet thinks that your party ought to be ready to move into the American Legation on instant notice, if you can't get away to sea to-morrow."

"What's the use, if the legation has no official existence?" asked Mr. Brewster.

"In a sense it has. It would probably be respected by a mob. And, at the worst, it adjoins the British Legation, which would be quite safe. If it weren't that Sir Willet's boy has typhoid, you'd be formally invited to go there."

"It's very good of you," said Miss Polly warmly. "But surely it would be an awful nuisance to you."

"On the contrary, you'd brace up my far-too-casual old housekeeper and get the machinery running. She constantly takes advantage of my bachelor ignorance.

If you say you'll come, I'll almost pray for the outbreak."

"Certainly we'll come, at any time you notify us," said Mr. Brewster. "And we're very grateful. Shall you have room for Mr. Carroll, too?"

"By all means. And I've notified Mr. Cluff. You won't mind his being there? He's a rough diamond, but a thoroughly decent fellow."

"Useful, too, in case of trouble, I should judge," said the magnate. "Then I'll wait for further word from you."

"Yes. I've got my men out on watch."

"Wouldn't it be - er - advisable for us to arm ourselves?"

"By no means! There's just one course to follow; keep the peace at any price, and give the Hochwaldians not the slightest peg on which to hang a charge that Americans have been responsible for any trouble that might arise. May I ask you," he added significantly, "to make this clear to Mr. Carroll?"

"Leave that to me," said Miss Brewster, with superb confidence.

"Content, indeed! You'll find our locality very pleasant, Miss Brewster. Three of the other legations are on the same block, not including the Hochwaldian, which is a quarter of a mile down the hill. On our corner is a house where several of the English railroad men live, and across is the Club Amicitia, made up largely of the jeunesse doree, who are mostly pro-American. So you'll be quite surrounded by friends, not to say adherents."

"Call on me to housekeep for you at any time," cried Polly gayly. "I'll begin to roll up my sleeves as soon as I get dressed to-morrow."

IX

THE BLACK WARNING

That weird three-part drama in the plaza which had so puzzled Miss Polly Brewster had developed in this wise: -

Coincidently with the departure of Preston Fairfax Fitzhugh Carroll from the hotel in his cab, the Unspeakable Perk emerged from a store near the far corner of the square, which exploited itself in the purest Castilian as offering the last word in the matter of gentlemen's apparel. "Articulos para Caballeros" was the representation held forth upon its signboard.

If it had articled Mr. Perkins, it must be confessed that it had done its job unevenly, not to say fantastically. His linen was fresh and new, quite conspicuously so, and, therefore, in sharp contrast to the frayed and patched, but scrupulously clean and neatly pressed khaki suit, which set forth rather bumpily his solid figure. A serviceable pith helmet barely overhung the protrusive goggles. His hands were encased in white cotton gloves, a size or two too large. Dismal buff spots on the palms impaired their otherwise virgin purity. As the wearer carried his hands stiffly splayed, the blemishes were obtrusive. Altogether, one might have said that, if he were going in for farce, he was appropriately made up for it.

At the corner above the beggar's niche he was turning toward a pharmacist's entrance, when the mirth of the departing crowd that had been enjoying the free oratory attracted his attention. He glanced across at the beggar, now rocking rhythmically on his stumps, hesitated a moment, then ran down the steps.

At the same moment Carroll's cab stopped on the other angle of the curb. The occupant put forth his head, saw the goggled freak descending to the legless freak, and sat back again.

"Hola, Pancho! Are you ill?" asked the newcomer.

The beggar only swung back and forth, muttering with frenzied rapidity. With one hand the Unspeakable Perk stopped him, as one might intercept the runaway pendulum of a clock, setting the other on his forehead. Then he bent and brought his goblin eyes to bear on the dark face. The features were distorted, the eyelids tremulous over suffused eyes, and the teeth set. Opening the man's loose shirt, Perkins thrust his hand within. It might have been supposed that he was feeling for the heart action, were it not that his hand slid past the breast and around under the arm. When he drew it out, he stood for a moment with chin dropped, in consideration.

Midday heat had all but cleared the plaza. As he looked about, the helper saw no aid, until his eye fell upon the waiting cab. He fairly bounded up the stairs, calling something to the coachman.

" No , " grunted that toiler , with   the   characteristic

discourtesy of the Caracunan lower class, and jerked his head backward toward his fare.

"I beg your pardon," said the Unspeakable Perk eagerly, in Spanish, turning to the dim recess of the victoria. "Might I - Oh, it's you!" He seized Carroll by the arm. "I want your cab."

"Indeed!" said Carroll. "Well, you're cool enough about it."

"And your help," added the other.

"What for?"

" Do you have to ask questions? The man may be dying - is dying, I think."

"All right," said Carroll promptly. "What's to be done?"

"Get him home. Help me carry him to the cab."

Between them, the two men lifted the heavy, mumbling cripple, carried him up the steps with a rush, and deposited him in the cab, while the driver was still angrily expostulating. The beggar was shivering now, and the cold sweat rolled down his face. His bearers placed themselves on each side of him. Perkins gave an order to the driver, who seemed to object, and a rapid-fire argument ensued.

"What's wrong?" asked Carroll.

"Says he won't go there. Says he was hired by you for shopping."

Carroll took one look at the agony-wrung face of the beggar, who was being held on the seat by his companion.

"Won't he?" said he grimly. "We'll see."

Rising, he threw a pair of long arms around those of the driver, pinning him, caught the reins, and turned the horses.

"Now ask him if he'll drive," he directed Perkins.

"Si, senor!" gasped the coachman, whose breath had been squeezed almost through his crackling ribs.

"See that you do," the Southerner bade him, in accents that needed no interpretation.

Presently Perkins looked up from his charge.

"Got a cigar?" he asked abruptly.

"No," replied the other, a little disgusted by this levity in the presence of imminent death.

Perkins bade the driver stop at the corner.

"Don't let him fall off the seat," he admonished Carroll, and jumped out.

In the course of a minute he reappeared, smoking a cheroot that appeared to be writhing and twisting in the effort to escape from its own noxious fumes.

"Have one," he said, extending a handful to his companion.

"I don't care for it," returned the other superciliously. While willing to aid in a good work, he did not in the least approve either of the Unspeakable Perk or of his offhand manners.

Before they had gone much farther, his resentment was heated to the point of offense.

"Is it necessary for you to puff every puff of that infernal smoke in my face?" he demanded ominously.

"Well, you wouldn't smoke, yourself."

"If it weren't for this poor devil of a sick man - " began Carroll, when a second thought about the smoke diverted his line of thought. "Is it contagious?" he asked.

"It's so regarded," observed the other dryly.

"I'll take one of those, thank you."

Perkins handed him one of the rejected spirals. In silence, except for the outrageous rattling of the wheels on the cobbles, they drove through mean streets that grew ever meaner, until they drew up at the blind front of a building abutting on an arroyo of the foothills. Here they stopped, and Carroll threw his jehu a five-bolivar piece, which the driver caught, driving away at once, without the demand for more which usually follows overpayment in Caracuna. Convenient to hand lay a small rock. Perkins used it for a knocker, hammering on the guarded wooden door with such vehemence as to still the clamor that arose from within.

Through the opening, as the barrier was removed by a leather-skinned old crone, Carroll gazed into a passageway, beyond which stretched a foul mule yard, bordered by what the visitor at first supposed to be stalls, until he saw bedding and utensils in them. The two men lifted the cripple in, amid the outcries and lamentations of the aged woman, who had looked at his face and then covered her own. At once they were surrounded by a swarm of women and children, who pressed upon them, hampering their movements, until a shrill voice cried: -

"La muerte negra!"

The swarm fell into silence, scattered, vanished, leaving only the moaning woman to help. At her direction they settled the patient on a straw pallet in a side room.

"That's all you can do," said the Unspeakable Perk to his companion. "And thank you."

"I'll stay."

The goggles gloomed upon him in the dim room.

"I thought probably you would," commented Perkins, and busied himself over the cripple with a knife and some cloths. He had stuffed his ludicrous white gloves into his pocket, and was tearing strips from his handkerchief with skillful fingers.

"Oughtn't he to have a doctor?" asked Carroll. "Shall I go for one?"

"His mother has sent. No use, though."

"He can't be saved?"

"Not a chance on earth. I should say he was in the last stages."

"What is it?" said Carroll hesitantly.

"La muerte negra. The black death."

"Plague?"

"Yes."

"Are you sure? Are you an expert?"

"One doesn't have to be to recognize a case like that. The lump in the armpit is as big as a pigeon's egg."

"Why have you interested yourself in the man to such an extent?" asked Carroll curiously.

"He's a friend of mine. Why did you?"

"Oh, that's quite different. One can't disregard a call for help such as yours."

"A certain kind of 'one' can't," returned the Unspeakable Perk, with his half-smile. "You don't mind my saying, Mr. Carroll, you're a brave man."

"And I'd have said that you weren't," replied the other bluntly. "I give it up. But I know this: I'm going to be pretty wretchedly frightened until I know that I haven't got it. I'm frightened now."

"Then you're a braver man than I thought. But the

danger may be less than you think. Stick to that cigar - here are two more - and wait for me outside. Here's the doctor."

Profound and solemn under a silk hat, the local physician entered, bowing to Carroll as they passed in the hallway. Almost immediately Perkins emerged. On his face was a sardonic grin.

"Malaria," he observed. "The learned professor assures me that it's a typical malaria."

"Then it isn't the plague," said Carroll, relieved.

His relief was of brief duration.

"Of course it's plague. But if Professor Silk Hat, in there, officially declared it such, he'd have bracelets on his arms in twelve hours. The present Government of Caracuia doesn't believe in bubonic plague. I fancy our unfortunate friend in there will presently disappear, either just before or just after death. It doesn't greatly matter."

"What is to be done now?" asked Carroll.

"See that brush fire up there?" The hermit pointed to the hillside. "If we steep ourselves in that smoke until we choke, I think it will discourage any fleas that may have harbored on us. The flea is the only agent of communication."

Soot-begrimed, strangling, and with streaming eyes, they emerged, five minutes later, from the cloud of smoke. From his pocket the Unspeakable Perk dragged forth his white gloves. The action attracted his companion's attention.

"Good Lord!" he cried. "What has happened to your hands?"

"They're blistered."

"Stripped, rather. They look as if you'd fallen into a fire, or rowed a fifty-mile race. That message of Mr. Brewster's - See here, Perkins, you didn't row that over to the mainland? No, you couldn't. That's absurd. It's too far."

"No; I didn't row it to the mainland."

"But you've been rowing. I'd swear to those hands. Where? The blockading Dutch warship?"

The other nodded.

"Last night. Yah-h-h!" he yawned. "It makes me sleepy to think of it."

"Why didn't they blow you out of the water?" "Oh, I was semiofficially expected. Message from our consul. They transferred the message by wireless. I'm telling you all this, Mr. Carroll, because I think you'll get your release within forty-eight hours, and I want you to see that some of your party keeps constantly in touch with Mr. Sherwen. It's mighty important that your party should get out before plague is officially declared."

"Are you going to report this case?"

"All that I know about it."

"But, of course, you can't report officially, not being a physician," mused the other. "Still, when Dr. Pruyn comes, it will be evidence for him, won't it?"

"Undoubtedly. I should consider any delay after twenty-four hours risky for your party."

"What shall you do? Stay?"

"Oh, I've my place in the mountains. That's remote enough to be safe. Thank Heaven, there's a cloud over the sun! Let's sit down by this tree for a minute."

Unthinkingly, as he stretched himself out, the Unspeakable Perk pushed his goggles back and presently slipped them off. Thus, when Carroll, who had been gazing at the mist-capped peak of the mountain in front, turned and met his companion's eyes, he underwent something of the same shock that Polly Brewster had experienced, though the nature of his sensation was profoundly different. But his impression of the suddenly revealed face was the same. Ribbed-in though his mind was with tradition, and distorted with falsely focused ideals and prejudices, Preston Fairfax Fitzhugh Carroll possessed a sound underlying judgment of his fellow man, and was at bottom a frank and honorable gentleman. In his belief, the suddenly revealed face of the man beside him came near to being its own guaranty of honor and good faith.

"By Heavens, I don't believe it!" he blurted out, his gaze direct upon the Unspeakable Perk.

"What don't you believe?"

"That rotten club gossip."

"About me?"

"Yes," said Carroll, reddening.

The hermit pushed his glasses down, settled into place the white gloves, with their soothing contents of emollient greases, and got to his feet.

"We'd best be moving. I've got much to do," he said.

"Not yet," retorted Carroll. "Perkins, is there a woman up there on the mountains with you?"

"That is purely my own business."

"You told Miss Brewster there wasn't. If you tell me -"

"I never told her any such thing. She misunderstood."

"Who is the woman?"

"If you want it even more frankly, that is none of your concern."

"You have been letting Miss Brewster -"

"Are you engaged to marry Miss Brewster?"

"No."

"Then you have no authority to question me. But," he added wearily, "if it will ease your mind, and because of what you've done to-day, I 'll tell you this - that I do not expect ever to see Miss Brewster again."

" That isn't enough , " insisted Carroll , his face

darkening. "Her name has already been connected with yours, and I intend to follow this through. I am going to find out who the woman is at your place."

"How do you propose to do it?"

"By coming to see."

"You'll be welcome," said the other grimly. "By the way, here's a map." He made a quick sketch on the back of an envelope. "I'll be there at work most of to-morrow. Au revoir." He rose and started down the hill. "Better keep to yourself this evening," he warned. "Take a dilute carbolic bath. You'll be all right, I think."

Slowly and thoughtfully the Southerner made his way back to the hotel. After dining in his own room, he found time heavy on his hands; so, dispatching a note of excuse to Miss Brewster on the plea of personal business, he slipped out into the city. Wandering idly toward the hills, he presently found himself in a familiar street, and, impelled by human curiosity, proceeded to turn up the hill and stop opposite the blank door.

Here he was puzzled. To go in and inquire, even if he cared to and could make himself understood, would perhaps involve further risk of infection. While he was considering, the door slowly opened, and the leather-skinned crone appeared. Her eyes were swollen. In her hand she carried a travesty of a wreath, done in whitish metal, which she had interwoven with her own black mantilla, the best substitute for crape at hand. This she undertook to hang on the door. As Carroll crossed to address her, a powerful, sullen-faced man, with a scarred forehead and the insignia of some official status, apparently civic, on his coat, emerged from a doorway and addressed her harshly. She raised her reddened eyes to him and seemed to be pleading for permission to set up the little tribute to her dead. There was the exchange of a few more words. Then, with an angry exclamation, the official snatched the wreath from her. Carroll's hand fell on his shoulder. The man swung and saw a stranger of barely half his bulk, who addressed him in what seemed to be politely remonstrant tones. He shook himself loose and threw the wreath in the crone's face. Then he went down like a log under the impact of a swinging blow behind the ear. With a roar he leaped up and rushed. The foreigner met him with right and left, and this time he lay still.

Hanging the tragically unsightly wreath on the door, through which the terrified mourner had vanished, Carroll returned to the Gran Hotel Kast, his perturbed and confused thoughts and emotions notably relieved by that one comforting moment of action.

X

THE FOLLY OF PERK

Of the comprehensive superiority of the American Legation over the Gran Hotel Kast there could be no shadow of a doubt. From the moment of their arrival at noon of the day after the British Minister's warning, the refugees found themselves comfortable and content, Miss Brewster having quietly and tactfully taken over the management of internal affairs and reigning, at Sherwen's request, as generalissima. No disturbance had marked the transfer to their new abode. In fact, so wholly lacking was any evidence of hostility to the foreigners on the part of the crowds on the streets that the Brewsters rather felt themselves to be extorting hospitality on false pretenses. Sherwen, however, exhibited signal relief upon seeing them safely housed.

"Please stay that way, too," he requested.

"But it seems so unnecessary, and I want to market," protested Miss Polly.

"By no means! The market is the last place where any of us should be seen. It is in that section that Urgante has been doing his work."

"Who is he?"

"A wandering demagogue and cheap politician. Abuse of the 'Yankis' is his stock in trade. Somebody has been furnishing him money lately. That's the sole fuel to his fires of oratory."

"Bet the bills smelled of sauerkraut when they reached him," grunted Cluff, striding over to the window of the drawing-room, where the informal conference was being held.

"They may have had a Hochwaldian origin," admitted Sherwen. "But it would be difficult to prove."

"At least the Hochwald Legation wouldn't shed any tears over a demonstration against us," said Carroll.

"Well within the limits of diplomatic truth," smiled the American official.

"Pooh!" Mr. Brewster puffed the whole matter out of consideration. "I don't believe a word of it. Some of my acquaintances at the club, men in high governmental positions, assure me that there is no anti-American feeling here."

"Very likely they do. Frankness and plain-speaking being, as you doubtless know, the distinguishing mark of the Caracunan statesman."

The sarcasm was not lost upon Mr. Brewster, but it failed to shake his skepticism.

"There are some business matters that require that I should go to the office of the Ferro carril del Norte this afternoon," he said.

"I beg that you do nothing of the sort," cried Sherwen sharply.

The magnate hesitated. He glanced out of the window and along the street, close bounded by blank-walled houses, each with its eyes closed against the sun. A solitary figure strode rapidly across it.

"There's that bug-hunting fellow again," said Mr. Brewster. "He's an American, I guess, - God save the mark! Nobody seems to be interfering with HIM, and he's freaky enough looking to start a riot on Broadway."

Further comment was checked by the voice of the scientist at the door, asking to see Mr. Sherwen at once. Miss Polly immediately slipped out of the room to the patio, followed by Carroll and Cluff.

"My business, probably," remarked Mr. Brewster. "I'll just stay and see." And he stayed.

So far as the newcomer was concerned, however, he might as well not have been there; so he felt, with unwonted injury. The scientist, disregarding him wholly, shook hands with Sherwen.

"Have you heard from Wisner yet?"

"Yes. An hour ago."

"What was his message?"

"All right, any time to-day."

"Good! Better get them down to-night, then, so they can start to-morrow morning."

"Will Stark pass them?"

"Under restrictions. That's all been seen to."

At this point it appeared to Mr. Brewster that he had figured as a cipher quite long enough.

"Am I right in assuming that you are talking of my party's departure?" he inquired.

"Yes," said Sherwen. "The Dutch will let you through the blockade."

"Then my cablegram reached the proper parties at Washington," said the magnate, with an I-knew-it-would-be-that-way air.

"Thanks to Mr. Perkins."

"Of course, of course. That will be - er - suitably attended to later."

The Unspeakable Perk turned and regarded him fixedly; but, owing to the goggles, the expression was indeterminable.

"The fact is it would be more convenient for me to go day after to-morrow than to-morrow."

"Then you'd better rent a house," was the begoggled one's sharp and brief advice.

"Why so?" queried the great man, startled.

"Because if you don't get out to-morrow, you may not get out for months."

"As I understand the Dutch permit, it specifies AFTER to-day."

"It isn't a question of the Dutch. Caracuna City goes under quarantine to-night, and Puerto del Norte to-morrow, as soon as proper official notification can be given."

"Then plague has actually been found?"

"Determined by bacteriological test this morning."

"How do you know?"

"I was present at the finding."

"Who did it? Dr. Pruyn?"

The other nodded.

Sherwen whistled.

"Better make ready to move, Mr. Brewster," he advised. "You can't get out of port after quarantine is on. At least, you couldn't get into any other port, even if you sailed, because your sailing-master wouldn't have clearance papers."

The magnate smiled.

"I hardly think that any United States Consul, with a due regard for his future, would refuse papers to the yacht Polly," he observed.

"Don't be a fool!"

Thatcher Brewster all but jumped from his chair. That this adjuration should have come from the freakish spectacle-wearer seemed impossible. Yet Sherwen, the only other person in the room, was certainly not guilty.

"Did you address me, young man?"

"I did."

"Do you know, sir, that since boyhood no person has dared or would dare to call me a fool?"

"Well, I don't want to set a fashion," said the other equably. "I'm only advising you not to be."

"Keep your advice until it's wanted."

"If it were a question of you alone, I would. But there are others to be considered. Now, listen, Mr. Brewster: Wisner and Stark wouldn't let you through that quarantine, after it's declared, if you were the Secretary himself. A point is being stretched in giving you this chance. If you'll agree to ship a doctor, - Stark will find you one, - stay out for six full days before touching anywhere, and, if plague develops, make at once for any detention station specified by the doctor, you can go. Those are Stark's conditions."

"Damnable nonsense!" declared Mr. Brewster, jumping to his feet, quite red in the face.

"Let me warn you, Mr. Brewster," put in Sherwen, with quiet force, "that you are taking a most unwise course. I am advised that Mr. Perkins is acting under instructions from our consulate."

"You say that Dr. Pruyn is here. I want to see him before -"

"How can you see him? Nobody knows where he is keeping himself. I haven't seen him yet myself. Now, Mr. Brewster, just sit down and talk this over reasonably with Mr. Perkins."

"Oh, no," said the third conferee positively; "I've no time for argument. At six o'clock I 'll be back here. Unless you decide by then, I'll telephone the consulate that the whole thing is off."

"Of all the impudent, conceited, self-important young whippersnappers!" fumed Mr. Brewster. But he found that he had no audience, as Sherwen had followed the scientist out of the room.

Before the afternoon was over, the American concessionnaire had come to realize that the situation was less assured than he had thought. Twice the British Minister had come, and there had been calls from the representatives of several other nationalities. Von Plaanden, in full uniform and girt with the short saber that is the special and privileged arm of the crack cavalry regiment to which he belonged at home, had dismounted to deliver personally a huge bouquet for Miss Brewster, from the garden of the Hochwald Legation, not even asking to see the girl, but merely leaving the flowers as a further expression of his almost daily apology, and riding on to an official review at the military park.

He had spoken vaguely to Sherwen of a restless

condition of the local mind. Reports, it appeared, had been set afloat among the populace to the effect that an American sanitary officer had been bribed by the enemies of Caracuna to declare plague prevalent, in order to close the ports and strangle commerce. Urgante was going about the lower part of the city haranguing on street corners without interference from the police. In the arroyo of the slaughter-house, two American employees of the street-car company had been stoned and beaten. Much aguardiente was in process of consumption, it being a half-holiday in honor of some saint, and nobody knew what trouble might break out.

"Bolas are rolling around like balls on a billiard table," said young Raimonda, who had come after luncheon to call on Miss Brewster. "In this part of the city there will be nothing. You needn't be alarmed."

"I'm not afraid," said Miss Polly.

"I'm sure of it," declared the Caracunan, with admiration. "You are very wonderful, you American women."

"Oh, no. It's only that we love excitement," she laughed.

"Ah, that is all very well, for a bull-fight or 'la boxe.' But for one of our street emeutes - no; too much!"

They were seated on the roof of the half-story of the house, which had been made into a trellised porch overlooking the patio in the rear and the street in front, an architectural wonder in that city of dead walls flush with the sidewalk line all the way up. Leaning over the rail, the visitor pointed through the leaves of a small gallito tree to a broad-fronted building almost opposite.

"That is my club. You have other friends there who would do anything for you, as I would, so gladly," he added wistfully. "Will you honor me by accepting this little whistle? It is my hunting-whistle. And if there should be anything - but I think there will not - you will blow it, and there will be plenty to answer. If not, you will keep it, please, to remember one who will not forget you."

Handsome and elegant and courtly he was, a true chevalier of adventurous pioneering stock, sprung from the old proud Spanish blood, but there stole behind the girl's vision, as she bade him farewell, the undesired phantasm of a very different face, weary and lined and lighted by steadfast gray eyes - eyes that looked truthful and belonged to a liar! Miss Polly Brewster resumed her final packing in a fume of rage at herself.

All hands among the visitors passed the afternoon dully. Mr. Brewster, who had finally yielded to persuasion and decided not to venture out, though still deriding the restriction as the merest nonsense, was in a mood of restless silence, which his irrepressible daughter described to Fitzhugh Carroll as "the superior sulks."

Carroll himself kept pretty much aloof. He had the air of a man who wrestles with a problem. Cluff fussed and fretted and privately cursed the country and all its concessions. Between calls and the telephone, Sherwen was kept constantly busy. But a few minutes before six, central, in the blandest Spanish, regretted to inform him that Puerto del Norte was cut off. When would service be resumed? Quien sabe'? It was an order. Hasta manana. To-morrow, perhaps. Smoothing a furrow from his brow, the sight of which would have done nobody any good, he suggested that they all gather on the roof porch for a swizzle. The suggestion was hailed with enthusiasm.

Thus, when the Unspeakable Perk came hustling down the street some minutes earlier than the appointed time, he was hailed in Sherwen's voice, and bidden to come directly up. No time, on this occasion, for Miss Polly to escape. She decided in one breath to ignore the man entirely; in the next to bow coldly and walk out; in the next to - He was there before the latest wavering decision could be formulated.

"Better all get inside," he said a little breathlessly. "There may be trouble."

Cluff brightened perceptibly.

"What kind of trouble?"

"Urgante is leading a mob up this way. They're turning the corner now."

"I'm going to wait and see them," cried Miss Polly, with decision.

"Bend over, then, all of you," ordered Sherwen. "The vines will cover you if you keep down."

Around the corner, up the hill from where they were, streamed a rabble of boys, leaping and whooping, and after them a more compact crowd of men, shoeless, centering on a tall, broad, heavy-mustached fellow who bore on a short staff the Stars and Stripes.

"Where on earth did he get that?" cried Sherwen.

"Looted the Bazaar Americana," replied Perkins.

"That's Urgante," growled Cluff; "that devil with the flag."

"But he seems to be eulogizing it," cried the girl.

The orator had set down his bright burden, wedging it in the iron guard railing of a tree, and was now apostrophizing it with extravagant bows and honeyed accents in which there was an undertone of hiss. For confirmation, Miss Polly turned to the others. The first face her eyes fell on was that of the ball-player. Every muscle in it was drawn, and from the tightened lips streamed such whispered curses as the girl never before had heard. Next him stood the hermit, solid and still, but with a queer spreading pallor under his tan. In front of them Sherwen was crouched, scowlingly alert. The expression of Mr. Brewster and Carroll, neither of whom understood Spanish, betokened watchful puzzlement.

Enlightenment burst upon them the next minute. From the motley crowd below rose a snarl of laughter and savage jeering, the object of which was unmistakable.

"By G - d!" cried Mr. Brewster, straightening up and grasping the railing. "They're insulting the flag!"

"I've left my pistol!" muttered Carroll, white-lipped. "I've left my pistol!"

Polly Brewster's hand flew to her belt.

She drew out the automatic and held it toward the Southerner. But it was not Carroll's hand that met hers; it was the Unspeakable Perk's.

"No," said he, and he flung the weapon back of him into the patio.

"Oh! Oh!" cried the girl. "You unspeakable coward!"

Carroll jumped forward, but Sherwen was equally quick. He interposed his slight frame.

"Perkins is right," he said decisively. "No shooting. It would be worth the life of every one here. We've got to stand it. But somebody is going to sweat blood for this day's work!"

The instinct of discipline, characteristic of the professional athlete, brought Cluff to his support.

"What Mr. Sherwen says, goes," he said, almost choking on the words. "We've got to stand it."

In the breast of Miss Polly Brewster was no response to this spirit. She was lawless with the lawlessness of unconquered youth and beauty.

"Oh!" she breathed "If I had my pistol back, I'd shoot that BEAST myself!"

The scientist turned his goggles hesitantly upon her.

"Miss Brewster," he began, "please don't think -"

"Don't speak to me!" she cried.

Another clamor of derision sounded from the street as Urgante resumed the standard of his mockery and led his rabble forward. Behind the dull-colored mass appeared a spot of splendor. It was Von Plaanden, gorgeous in his full regalia, who had turned the corner, returning from the public reception. Well back of the mob, he pulled his horse up, and sat watching. The coincidence was unfortunate. It seemed to justify Sherwen's bitter words: -

"Come to visa his work. There's the Hochwaldian for you!"

Forward danced and reeled the "Yanki" baiters below, until they were under the balcony where the little group of Americans sheltered and raged silently. There the orator again spewed forth his contempt upon the alien banner, and again the ranks behind him shrieked their approval of the affront. Miss Polly Brewster, American of Americans, whose great-grandfathers had fought with Herkimer and Steuben, - themselves the sons of women who had stood by the loopholes of log houses and caught up the rifles of their fallen pioneer husbands, wherewith to return the fire of the besieging Mohawks, - ran forward to the railing, snatching her skirt from the detaining grasp of her father. In the corner stood a huge bowl of roses. Gathering both hands full, she leaned forward and flung them, so that they fell in a shower of loveliness upon the insulted flag of her nation.

For an instant silence fell upon the "great unwashed" below. Out of it swelled a muttering as the leader made a low, mocking obeisance to the girl, following it with a word that brought a jubilant yelp from his adherents. Stooping, he ladled up in his cupped hand a quantity of gutter filth. Where the flowers had but a moment before fluttered in the folds, he splotched it, smearing star, bar, and blue with its blackness. At the sight, the girl burst into helpless tears, and so stood weeping, openly, bitterly, and unashamed.

No brain is so well ordered, no emotion so thoroughly controlled, but that under sudden pressure - click! - the mechanism slips a cog and runs amuck. Just that thing happened inside the Unspeakable Perk's smooth-running, scientific brain upon incitement of his flag's desecration and his lady's grief. To her it seemed that he shot past her horizontally like a human dart. The next second he was over the railing, had swung from a branch of the neighboring tree to the trunk, and leaped to the ground, all in one movement of superhuman agility. To the mob his exploit was apparently without immediate significance. Perhaps they didn't notice the descent; or perhaps those few who saw were so astonished at the apparition of a chunky tree-man with protuberant eyes scrambling down upon them in the manner of an ape, that they failed to appreciate what it might portend of trouble.

The hermit landed solidly on his feet a few yards from Urgante, the flag bearer. With a berserker yell, he rushed. Taken by surprise, the assailed one still had time to lift the heavy staff. As quickly, the American lowered his head and dove. It may not have been magnificent; it certainly was not war by the rules; but it was eminently effective. To say that the leader went down would be absurdly inadequate. He simply crumpled. Over and over he rolled on the cobbles, while the smirched flag flew clear of his grasp, and fell on the farther sidewalk.

"Wow!" yelled Cluff, leaping into the air. "Football! That cost him a couple of ribs. Hey, Rube!"

And he rushed for the stairs, followed by Carroll, Sherwen, and, only one jump behind, Mr. Thatcher Brewster, cursing in a manner that did credit to his patriotism, but would have added no luster to his record as an elder of the Pioneer Presbyterian Church, of Utica, New York.

Meantime, the Unspeakable Perk, having rolled free of the fallen enemy, staggered to his feet and caught up the flag. Stunned surprise on the part of the crowd gave him an instant's time. He edged along the curb, hoping to gain the legation door by a rush. But the foe threw out a wing, cutting him off. Several eager followers had lifted Urgante, whose groans and curses suggested a sound basis for Cluff's diagnosis. Himself quite hors de combat, he spat at the Unspeakable Perk, and cried upon his henchmen to kill the "Yanki." It seemed not improbable to the latter that they would do it. Perkins set his back to the wall, twirled the flag folds tight around the pole, reversed and clubbed the staff, and prepared to make any attempt at killing as uncomfortable and unprofitable as possible. The rabble, by no means favorably impressed by these businesslike proceedings, stood back, growling.

A hand flew up above the crowd. The Unspeakable Perk ducked sharply and just in time, as a knife struck the wall above him and clattered to the pavement. Instantly he caught it up, but the blade had snapped off short. As he stooped, one bold spirit rushed in. Perkins met him with a straight lance-thrust of the staff, which

Samuel Hopkins Adams

sent him reeling and shrieking with pain back to his fellows. But now another knife, and another, struck and fell from the wall at his back; badly aimed both, but presumably the forerunners of missiles, some of which would show better marksmanship. The assailed man cast a swift, desperate look about him; the crowd closed in a little. Obviously he must keep "eyes front."

"To your left! To your left!" The voice came to him clear and sweet above the swelling growl of the rabble. "The doorway! Get into the doorway, Mr. Beetle Man."

A few paces away, how far Perkins could only guess, was the entrance to the house. He surmised that, like many of the better-class houses, it had a small set-in door, at right angles to the main entrance, that would serve as a shallow shelter. Without raising his eyes, he nodded comprehension, and began to edge along the wall, swinging his stout weapon. As he went, he wondered what was keeping the others. At that moment the others were frantically wrestling with the all-too-adequate bars with which Sherwen had reinforced the wide door.

Perkins, feeling with a cautious heel, found himself opposite the entry indicated by the voice. Turning, he darted into the narrow embrasure. Here he was comparatively safe from the missiles that were now coming from all directions. On the other hand, he now lacked room to swing his formidable club. The peons, with a shout, closed in to arm's length. Alone on her balcony, the girl turned her head away and cried aloud, hopelessly, for help. She wanted to close her ears against the bestial shouts of a mob trampling to death a defenseless man , but her arms were of lead. She listened and shivered.

Instead of the sound that she dreaded there came the ringing of hoofs on stones, followed by yells of alarm. She opened her eyes to see Von Plaanden, bent forward in his saddle at the exact angle proper to the charge, urging his great horse down upon the mass of people as ruthlessly as if they had been so many insects. Through the circle he broke, swinging his mount around beside the shallow doorway before which three Caracunans already lay sprawled, attesting the vigor of the defender's final resistance. Back of the horseman lay half a dozen other figures. The Hochwaldian jerked out his sword and stood, a splendid spectacle. Very possibly he was not wholly unmindful of his own pictorial quality or of the lovely American witness thereto.

His intervention gave a few seconds' respite, one of those checks that save battles and make history. Now, in the further making of this particular history, sounded a lusty whoop from the opposite direction; such a battle slogan as only the Anglo-Saxon gives. It emanated from Galpy the bounder, bounding now, indeed, at full speed up the slope, followed by two of his fellow railroad men, flannel-clad and still perspiring from their afternoon's cricket. Against bare legs a cricket bat is a highly dissuasive argument. The Britons swung low and hard for the ancient right of the breed to break into a row wherever white men are in the minority against other races. The downhill wing of the mob being much the weakest, opened up for them with little resistance, leaving them a free path to the cavalryman, to whose side Perkins, with staff ready brandished, had advanced from his shelter.

"Wot's the merry game?" inquired the cockney cheerfully.

Before them the crowd swayed and parted, and there appeared, lifted by many arms, a figure with a dead-white face streaked with blood, running from a great gash in the scalp.

"He went down in front of my horse," explained the Hochwald secretary coolly.

At the sight, there rose from the crowd a wailing cry, quite different from its former voice. Galpy's teeth set and his cricket bat went up in the air.

"There'll be killing for this," he said. "I know these blightehs. That yell means blood. We must make a bolt for it. Is this all there is of us?"

At the moment of his asking, it was. One half a second later, it wasn't, as the last of the legation's stubborn bars yielded, the door burst open, and the four Americans tumbled out at the charge, Cluff yelling insanely, Carroll in deadly quiet, Sherwen alertly scanning the adversaries for identifiable faces, and Elder Brewster still imperiling his soul by the fervor of his language. Each was armed with such casual weapons as he had been able to catch up. Carroll, a leap in advance of the rest, encountered an Indian drover, half-dodged a swinging blow from his whip, and sent him down with a broken shoulder from a chop with a baseball club that he had found in the hallway. A bull-like charge had carried Cluff deep among the Caracunans, where he encountered a huge peon. whom he seized and flung bodily over the iron guard of a samon tree, where the man hung, yelling dismally.

Two other peons, who had seized the athlete around the knees, were all but brained by a stoneware gin bottle in the hands of Sherwen. Meanwhile, Mr. Brewster was performing prodigies with a niblick which he had extracted, at full run, from a bag opportunely resting against the hat-rack. Almost before they knew it, the rescue party had broken the intercepting wing of the mob, and had joined the others.

Cluff threw a gorilla-like arm across the Unspeakable Perk's shoulder,

"Hurt, boy?" he cried anxiously.

"No, I'm all right. Who's left with Miss Brewster?"

"Nobody. We must get back."

Sherwen's cool voice cut in: -

"Close together, now. Keep well up. Herr von Plaanden, will you cover us at the end?"

"It is the post of honor," said the Hochwaldian.

"You've earned it. But for you, they'd have got our colors."

The foreigner bowed, and swung his horse toward a Caracunan who had pressed forward a little too near. But, for the moment the fight had oozed out of the mob.

Without mishap the group got across the street, Perkins still clinging to the flag.

Suddenly, from the rear rank, came a shower of stones, followed by the final rush. Galpy and Perkins went down. Von Plaanden tottered in his saddle, but quickly recovered. Instantly Perkins was up again, the blood streaming from the side of his head. He was conscious of brown hands clutching at the cricketer, to drag him away. He himself seized the cockney's legs and braced for that absurd and deadly tug of war. Then Von Plaanden's saber descended, and he was able to haul Galpy back into safety.

The situation was desperate now. Mr. Brewster was pinned against the wall and disarmed, but still fighting with fist and foot. Half a dozen peons were struggling with Cluff across the bodies of as many more whom he had knocked down. Sherwen, almost under the cavalryman's mount, was protecting his rear with the fallen Galpy's cricket bat, and the two other cricketers were fighting back to back on the other side. Carroll was clubbing his way toward Mr. Brewster, but his weapon was now in his left hand. Matters looked dark indeed, when there shrilled fiercely from above them the whirring peal of a silver whistle.

Polly Brewster had remembered Raimonda. It seemed a futile signal, for as she ran to the railing and gazed across at the Club Amicitia, she saw all its windows and doors tight closed, as befits an aristocratic club that has no concern with the affairs of the rabble. But there is no way of closing a patio from the top, and sounds can enter readily that way, when all other apertures are shut. Long and loud Miss Polly blew the signal on the silver hunting-whistle.

In the club patio, Raimonda was chafing and wondering, and a score of his friends were drinking and waiting. That signal released their activities and terminated the battle of the American Legation most ingloriously for the forces of Urgante. For the gilded youth of Caracuna bears a heavy cane of fashion, and carries a ready revolver, also, although not so admittedly as a matter of fashion. Furthermore, he has a profound contempt for the peon class; a contempt extending to life and limb. Therefore, when some two dozen young patricians sallied abruptly forth with their canes, and the mob caught sight, here and there, of a glint of nickel against the black, it gave back promptly. Some desultory stones rattled against the walls. There were answering reports a few, and sundry yells of pain. The army of Urgante broke and fled down the side streets, leaving behind its broken and its wounded. Most of the bullet casualties were below the knee. The Caracunan aristocrat always fires low - the first time.

Shortly thereafter, Miss Polly Brewster appeared upon the balcony of the American Legation, and performed an illegal act. Upon a day not designated as a Caracunan national holiday, she raised the flag of an alien nation and fixed it, and the gilded youth of Caracuna in the street below cheered, not the flag, which would have been unpatriotic, but the flag-raiser, which was but gallant, until they were hoarse and parched of throat.

XI

PRESTO CHANGE

After the battle, Miss Brewster reviewed her troops, and took stock of casualties, in the patio. None of the allied forces had come off scatheless. Galpy, whose injuries had at first seemed the most severe, responded to a stiff dose of brandy. A cut across the scientist's head had been hastily bandaged in a towel, giving him, as he observed, the appearance of a dissipated Hindu. To Von Plaanden's indignant disgust, his military splendor was seriously impaired by a huge "hickey" over his left eye, the memento of a well-aimed rock. Cluff had broken a finger and sprained his wrist. Mr. Brewster was anxious to know if any one had seen two teeth of his on the pavement or whether he was to look for later digestive indications of their whereabouts. Both of the young cricketers had been battered and bruised, though it was nothing, they gleefully averred, to what they had meted out. And Carroll had a nasty-looking knife-thrust in his shoulder.

All of them were disheveled, dilapidated, and grimy to the last degree, except the Hochwaldian, who still sat his horse, which he had ridden into the patio. But Miss Polly said to herself, with a thrill of pride, that no woman need wish a more gallant and devoted band of defenders. Leaning over them from the inner railing of the balcony, she surveyed them with sparkling eyes.

"It was magnificent!" she cried. "Oh, I'm so proud of you all! I could hug you, every one!"

"Better come down from there, Polly," said her father anxiously. "Some of those ruffians might come back."

"Not to-day," said Sherwen grimly. "They've had enough."

"That is correct," confirmed Von Plaanden. "Nevertheless, there may be disorder later. Would it not be better that you go to the British Legation, Fraulein?"

"Not I!" she returned. "I stay by my colors. And now I'm going to disband my army."

Stretching out her hand to a vase near her, she drew out a rose of deepest red and held it above Von Plaanden.

"The color of my country," said Von Plaanden gravely. "May I take it for a sign that I am forgiven?"

"Fully, freely, and gladly," said the girl. "You have put a debt upon us all that I - that we can never repay."

"It is I who pay. You will not think of me too hardly, for my one breach?"

"I shall think of you as a hero," said the girl impetuously. "And I shall never forget. Catch, O knight."

The rose fell, and was caught. Von Plaanden bowed low over it. Then he straightened to the military salute, and so rode out of the door and out of the girl's life.

"Men are strange creatures," mused the philosopher of twenty. "You think they are perfectly horrid, and suddenly they show their other side to you, and you think they are perfectly splendid. I wish I knew a little more about real people."

She confessed to no more specific thought, but as she descended the stairs to bid farewell to the blushing and deprecatory Britons, she was eager to have it over with, and to come to speech with her beetle man, who had so strangely flamed into action. The Unspeakable Perk! As the name formed on her lips, she smiled tenderly. With sad lack of logic, she was ready to discard every suspicion of him that she had harbored, merely on the strength of his reckless outbreak of patriotism. She looked about the patio, but he was not there. Sherwen came out of a side door, his face puckered with anxiety.

"Where is Mr. Perkins?" she asked.

"In there." He nodded back over his shoulder. "Your father is with him. Perhaps you'd better go in."

With a chill at her heart, Polly entered the room, where Mr. Brewster bent a troubled face over a head swathed in reddened bandages.

Very crumpled and limp looked the Unspeakable Perk, bunched humpily upon the little sofa. His goggles had fallen off, and lay on the floor beside him, contriving somehow to look momentously solemn and important all by themselves. His face was turned half away, and, as Polly's gaze fell upon it, she felt again that queer catch at her heart.

"Wouldn't know it was the same chap, would you?" whispered Mr. Brewster.

The girl picked up the grotesque spectacles, cradling them for an instant in her hands before she put them aside and leaned over the quiet form.

"Came staggering in, and just collapsed down there," continued her father huskily. "Lord, I wouldn't lose that boy after this for a million dollars!"

"Why do you talk that way?" she demanded sharply. "What has happened? Did he faint?"

"Just collapsed. When I tried to rouse him, he kicked me in the chest," replied the magnate, with somber seriousness.

"Oh, you goose of a dad!" There was a tremulous note in Polly's low laughter. "That's all right, then. Can't you see he's dead for sleep, poor beetle man?"

"Do you think so?" said Mr. Brewster, vastly relieved. "Hadn't I better go out for a doctor, and make sure?"

She shook her head.

"Let him rest. Hand me that pillow, please, dad."

With soft little pushes and wedges she worked it under the scientist's head. "What a dreadful botch of bandaging! He looks so pale! I wonder if I couldn't get those cloths off. Lend me your knife, dad."

Gently as she worked, the head on the pillow began to sway, and the lips to move.

"Oh, let me alone!" they muttered querulously.

The eyes opened. The Unspeakable Perk gazed up into the faces above him, but saw only one, a face whose tender concern softened it to a loveliness greater even than when he had last seen it. He tried to rise, but the hands that pressed him back were firm and quick.

"Lie still!" bade their owner.

A thin film of color mounted to his cheeks.

"I - I - beg your pardon," he stammered. "I - I - d-didn't know -"

"Don't be a goose!" she adjured him. "It's only me."

"Yes, that's the trouble." He closed his eyes again, and began to murmur.

"What does he say?" asked Mr. Brewster, lowering his head and almost falling over backward as his astonished ears were greeted by the slowly intoned rhythm: -

"Scarab, tarantula, doodle-bug, flea."

"Delirious!" exclaimed the magnate. "Clean off his head! How does one find a doctor in this town?"

" No need, dad," his daughter reassured him. "It's just

a - a sort of game."

"Game! Did you hear what he said?"

"Well, a kind of password. It's all right, Dad. It is, really."

Still undecided, Mr. Brewster stared at the injured man.

"I don't know - " he began, when the eyes opened again.

"Feeling better?" inquired Polly briskly.

"Yes. The charm works perfectly."

"Anything I can do, or get, for you, my boy?" inquired Mr. Brewster, stepping forward.

"What's in the ice-box?" asked the other anxiously.

"Oh!" cried the girl in distress. "He's starving! When did you eat last?"

"I can't exactly remember. It was about five this morning, I think. A banana, and, as I recall it, a small one."

"Dad!" cried the girl, but that prompt and efficient gentleman was already halfway to the cook, dragging Sherwen along as interpreter.

"He'll get whatever there is in the shortest known time," the girl assured her patient. "Trust dad. Now, you lie back and let me fix up a fresh bandage."

"You'd have made a great trained nurse," he murmured, as she adjusted the clean strips that Sherwen had sent in. "Don't pin my ear down. It's got to help hold my goggles on."

"The dear funny goggles!" Picking them up, she patted them with dainty fingers, before setting them aside. He watched her uneasily, much in the manner of a dog whose bone has been taken away.

"Do you mind giving them back?" he said.

"But you're not going to wear them here," she protested.

"I've got so used to them," he explained apologetically, "that I don't feel really dressed without them."

She handed them back and he adjusted them to the bandages. "For the present, rest is prescribed you know," said she.

"Oh, no!" he declared. "As soon as I've had something to eat, I'll go. There are a hundred things to be done. Where are my gloves?"

"What gloves? Oh, those white abominations? Why on earth do you wear them?" Her glance fell upon his right hand, which lay half-open beside him. "Oh - oh - oh!" she cried in a rising scale of distress. "What have you done to your hands?"

He reddened perceptibly.

"Nothing."

"Nothing, indeed! Tell me at once!"

"I've been rowing."

"Where to?"

"Oh, out to a ship."

"There aren't any ships, except the Dutch warship. Was it to her?"

"Yes."

"To carry our message - MY message?"

He squirmed.

"I'm awfully sleepy," he protested. "It isn't fair to cross-examine a witness - "

"When was it?" his ruthless interrogator broke in.

"Night before last."

"How far?"

"How can I tell? Not far. A few miles."

"And back. And it took you all night," she accused.

"What if it did?" he cried peevishly. "A man's got to have some relief from work, hasn't he? It was livelier than sitting all night with one's eye glued to a microscope barrel!"

"Oh, beetle man, beetle man! I don't know about you at

all. What kind of a strange queer creature are you? Have you wings, Mr. Beetle Man?"

Suddenly she bent over and laid her soft lips upon the scarified palm. The Unspeakable Perk sat up, with a half-cry.

"Now the other one," said the girl. Her face was a mantle of rose-color, but her eyes shone.

"I won't! You shan't!"

"The other one!" she commanded imperiously.

"Please, Miss Brewster -"

A noise at the door saved him. There stood Thatcher Brewster, magnate, multi-millionaire, and master of men, a huge tray in his hands.

"Beefsteak, fried potatoes, alligator pear, fresh bread, REAL butter, coffee, AND cake," he proclaimed jovially. "Not to mention a cocktail, which I compounded with my own skilled hands. Are you ready, my boy? Go!"

The Unspeakable Perk leaped from his couch.

"Food!" he cried. "Real American food! The perfume of it is a square meal."

"You're much gladder to see it than you were me," pouted Miss Polly.

"I'm not half as afraid of it," he admitted. "Mr. Brewster, your health."

"Here's to you, my boy. Now I'll leave you with your nurse, and make my final arrangements. We're off by special in the morning."

"That's fine!" said the scientist.

But Miss Polly Brewster caught the turn of his head in her direction, and saw that his fork had slackened in his hand. Something tightened around her heart.

As he went, her father considered her for a moment, and wondered. Never before had he seen such a look in her eyes as that which she had turned on the queer, vivid stranger so busily engaged at the tray. Polly, and this obscure scientist! After the kind of men whom the girl had known, enslaved, and eluded! Absurd! Yet if it were to be - Mr. Brewster reviewed the events of the afternoon - well, it might be worse.

"By the Lord Harry, he's a MAN, anyway!" decided Thatcher Brewster.

Meanwhile, the subject of his musings began to feel like a man once more, instead of like a lath. Having wrought havoc among the edibles, he rose with a sigh.

"If I could have one hour's sleep," he said mournfully, "I'd be fit as a cricket."

"You shall," said the girl. "Mr. Sherwen says he won't let you out of the house until it's dark. And that's fully an hour."

"I ought to be on my way back now."

"Back where? To your mountains?"

"Yes."

"You'd be recognized and attacked before you could get out of the city. I won't let you."

"That wouldn't do, for a fact. Perhaps it would be safer to wait. I've made enough trouble for one day by my blunder-headed thoughtlessness."

"Is that what you call rescuing the flag?"

"Oh, rescuing!" he said slightingly. "What difference does it make what vermin like that mob do? Just for a whim, to endanger all of you."

She stared at him in amaze and suspicion. But he was quite honest.

"MY whim," she reminded him.

"Yes; I suppose it was," he admitted thoughtfully. "When I saw you crying, I lost my head, and acted like a child."

"Then it was all my fault?"

"Oh, I don't say that. Certainly not. I'm master of my own actions. If I hadn't wanted -"

"But it was my fault this much, anyway, that you wouldn't have done it except for me."

"Yes; it was your fault to that extent," he said honestly. "I hope you don't mind my saying so."

"Oh, beetle man, beetle man!" She leaned forward, her

eyes deep-lit pools of mirth and mockery and some more occult feeling that he could not interpret. "Would it scare you quite out of your poor, queer wits if I were to HUG you? Don't call for help. I'm not really going to do it."

"I know you're not," said he dolefully. "But about that row, I want to set myself right. I'm no fool. I know it took a certain amount of nerve to go down there. And I was even proud of it, in a way. And when Von Plaanden turned and gave me the salute before he went away, I liked it quite a good deal."

"Did he do that? I love him for it!" cried the girl.

"But my point is this, that what I did wasn't sound common sense. Now if Carroll had done it, it would have been all right."

"Why for him and not for you?"

"Because those are his principles. They're not mine."

"I wish you weren't quite so contemptuous of poor Fitz. It seems hardly fair."

"Contemptuous of him? I'd give half my life to be in his place after to-morrow."

"Why?" There was a flutter in her throat as she put the question.

"Because he's going with you, isn't he?"

"So are you, if you will."

"I can't."

"Father won't go without you, I believe. Won't you come, if I ask you?"

"No."

"Work, I suppose," said the girl; "the work that you love better than anything in the world."

"You're wrong there." His voice was not quite steady now. "But it's work that has to have my first consideration now. And there is one special responsibility that I can't evade, for the present, anyway."

"And afterward?" She dared not look at him as she spoke.

"Ah, afterward. There's too much 'perhaps' in the afterward down here. We science grubbers on the outposts enlist for the term of the war," he said, smiling wanly.

"How can I - can we go and leave you here?" she demanded obstinately.

"Oh, give me a square meal once in a while, and a night's rest here and there, and I'll do well enough."

"Oh, dear! I forgot your sleep. Here I've been chattering like a magpie. Take off your coat and lie down on that sofa at once."

"Where shall I find you when I wake up?"

"Right where you leave me when you fall asleep."

"Oh, no! You mustn't wear yourself out watching over me."

"Hush! You're under orders. Give me the coat." She hung it on the back of a chair. "Not another word now. And I'll call you when time is up."

He closed his eyes, and the girl sat studying his face in the dim light, graving it deep on her inner vision, seeking to formulate some conception of the strange being so still and placid before her. How had she ever thought him ridiculous and uncouth? How had she ever dared to insult him by distrust? What did it matter what other men, estimating him by their own sordid standards, said of him? As if her thought had established a connection with his, he opened his eyes and sat up.

"I knew there was something I wanted to ask you," he said. "What did your 'Never, never, never' mean?"

"A foolish misunderstanding that I'm ashamed of."

"Was it that - that woman-gossip business?"

"Yes. I was stupid. Will you forgive me?"

"What is there to forgive? Some time, perhaps, you'll understand the whole thing."

"Please don't let's say anything more about it. I do understand."

This was not quite true. All that Polly Brewster knew was that, with those clear gray eyes meeting hers, she would have believed his honor clean and high against the world. The presence of the woman, even that dress fluttering in the wind, was susceptible of a hundred simple explanations.

"Ah, that's all right, then." There was relief in his tone. "Of course, in a place like this there is a lot of gossip and criticism. And when one runs counter to the general law - " "Counter to the law?"

"Yes. As a rule, I'm not 'beyond the pale of law,'" he said, smiling. "But down here one isn't bound by the same conventions as at home."

The girl's hand went to her throat in a piteous gesture.

"I - I - don't understand. I don't want to understand."

"There's got to be a certain broad-mindedness in these matters," he blundered on, with what seemed to her outraged senses an abominable jauntiness. "But the risk was small for me, and, of course, for her, anything was better than the other life. At that, I don't see how the truth reached you. What is it, Miss Polly?"

Rage, grief, and shame choked the girl's utterance.

Without a word, she ran from the room, leaving her companion a prey to troubled wonder.

In the patio, she turned sharply to avoid a group gathered around Galpy, who, with a patch over one eye, was trying to impart some news between gasps.

"Got it from the bulletin board of La Liberdad," he cried. "Killed; body gone; devil to pay all over the place."

"What's that?" demanded the Unspeakable Perk, running out, coatless and goggleless.

"There's been another riot, and Dr. Luther Pruyn is killed," explained Sherwen.

"Who says so?"

"Bulletin board - La Liberdad - just saw it," panted Galpy.

"Nonsense! It's a bola"

"The whole city is ringing with it. They say it was a plot to get him out of the way to stop quarantine. The Foreign Office is buzzing with inquiries, and Puerto del Norte is burning up the wires."

"Puerto del Norte! How did they hear?"

"Telephone, of course. I hear Wisner is coming up," said Sherwen.

"I've got to get a wire to the port at once," cried the scientist. "At once!"

"You! What for?"

"To stop off Wisner. To tell him it isn't so."

"You're excited, my boy," said Mr. Brewster kindly. "Better lie down again."

"It's true, right enough," said the Englishman. "Sir Willet's cochero saw the mob get him."

"When? Where?" asked Fitzhugh Carroll.

"Haven't got any details, but the Government admits it."

"I don't care if the President and his whole cabinet swear to it," vociferated the Unspeakable Perk. "It's a fake. How can I get Puerto del Norte, Mr. Sherwen?"

"You can't get it at all for any such purpose. How do you know it's a fake?"

"How do I know? Oh, dammit! I'M Luther Pruyn!"

He snatched off his glasses and faced them.

The little group stood petrified. Mr. Brewster was first to recover.

"Crazy, poor chap!" he said. "Luther Pruyn was my classmate."

"That's my father, Luther L."

"Proofs," said Sherwen sharply.

"In my coat pocket. In the room. Can I have your wire, Mr. Sherwen?"

"It's cut."

"Come to the railway wire," offered Galpy. "My eye! Wot a game!"

The two men ran out, the scientist leaving behind coat and goggles.

"It was our little mix-up that started the rumor," said Carroll thoughtfully. "Somebody recognized Perk - Dr. Pruyn."

"When his glasses fell off," said CLuff. "They're some disguise."

"He's Luther Pruyn, sure enough!" said Mr. Sherwen, emerging from the room. "Here's the proof." He held out an official-looking document. "An order from the Dutch Naval Office, made out in his name."

"What does it say?" asked Carroll.

"I'm not much of a hand at Dutch, but it seems to direct the blockading warship to receive Dr. Luther Pruyn and wife and convey them to Curacao."

"And wife!" exclaimed Cluff loudly. He whistled as a vent to his amazement. "That explains all the talk about a woman - a lady in his quinta on the mountains?"

"Apparently," said Carroll. "May I see that document, Mr. Sherwen?"

The American representative handed him the paper. As he was studying it, Galpy reentered, still scant of breath from excitement and haste. "He's gone back to the mountains," he announced. "Sent word for you to get to the port before dawn, if you have to walk. See Mr. Wisner there. He'll arrange everything."

"Will Mr. Perk - Dr. Pruyn be there?" asked Mr. Brewster.

"He didn't say."

"But he's gone without his coat!"

"And goggles," said Cluff.

"And his pass," added Sherwen.

"Trust him to come back for them when he gets ready. He's a rum josser for doing things his own way. Now, about the train." And Galpy outlined the plan of departure to the men, who, except Carroll, had gathered about him. The Southerner, unnoticed, had slipped into the room where the scientist's coat lay. Coming out by the lower door, he was intercepted by Miss Polly Brewster. He interpreted the misery in her face, and turned sick at heart with the pain of what it told him.

"You heard?" he asked.

She nodded. "Is it true? Did you see the permit yourself?"

"Yes. Here it is."

"I don't want to see it. It doesn't matter," she said, with utter weariness in her voice. "When do we leave? I want to go home. Send father to me, please, Fitz."

Mr. Brewster came to her, bearing the news that the sailing was set for the morrow.

"I'm glad to know that Dr. and Mrs. Pruyn are provided for," she remarked, so casually that the troubled father drew a breath of relief, concluding that he must have misinterpreted the girl's interest in the man behind the goggles.

On his way to the patio, he passed through the room where the scientist had lain. He came out looking perturbed.

"Has any one been in that room just now?" he asked Sherwen.

"Not that I've seen."

"The coat and the other things are not there."

Inquiry and search alike proved unavailing. Not until an hour later did they discover that Carroll had also disappeared. Sherwen found a note from him on the office desk: -

Please look after my luggage. Will join the others at the yacht to-morrow.

P. F. F. C.

XII

THE WOMAN AT THE QUINTA

Thanks to his rival's map, Carroll had little difficulty in finding the trail to the mountain quinta. A brilliant new moon helped to make easy the ascent. What course he would pursue upon his arrival he had not clearly defined to himself. That would depend largely upon the attitude of the man he was seeking. The flame of battle, still hot from the afternoon's melee, burned high in the Southerner's soul, for he was not of those whose spirit rapidly cools. Bitter resentment on behalf of Miss Polly Brewster fanned that flame. On one point he was determined: neither he nor the so-called Perkins should leave the mountain until he had had from the latter's own lips a full explanation.

Coming out into the open space, he got his first glimpse of the quinta. It was dark, except for one low light. From the farther side there came faintly to his ear a rhythmical sound, with brief intervals of quiet, as if some one hard at labor were stopping from time to time for breath. At that distance, Carroll could not interpret the sound, but some unidentified quality of it struck chill upon his fancy. Long experience in the woods had made him a good trailsman. He proceeded cautiously until he reached the edge of the clearing.

The sound had stopped now, but he thought he could hear heavy breathing from beyond the house. As he moved toward that side, a small but malevolent-looking snake slithered out from beneath a bush near by. Involuntarily he leaped aside. As he landed, a round pebble slipped under his foot. He flung up his arm. It met the low branch of a tree, and saved him a fall. But the thrashing of the leaves made a startling noise in the moonlit stillness. The snake went on about its business.

"Hola!" challenged a voice around the angle of the house.

Carroll recognized the voice. He stepped out of the shadows and strode across the open space. At the corner of the house he met the muzzle of a revolver pointing straight at the pit of his stomach. Back of it were the steady and now goggleless eyes of Luther Pruyn.

"I am unarmed," said Carroll.

"Ah, it's you!" said the other. He lowered his weapon, carefully whirled the cylinder to bring the hammer opposite an empty chamber, and dropped it in his pocket. "What do you want?"

"An explanation."

"Quite so," said the other coolly. "I'd forgotten that I invited you here. How long had you been watching me?"

"I saw you only when you came out from behind the house."

"And you wish to know about - about my companion in this place?" continued the other in an odd tone.

"Yes."

"Understand that I don't admit that you have the smallest right. But to clear up a situation which no longer exists, I'm ready to satisfy you. Come in."

He held open the door of the room where the lone light was burning. In the middle of the floor was spread a sheet, beneath which a form was outlined in grisly significance. Carroll's host lifted the cover.

The woman was white-haired, frail, and wrinkled. One side of her face shone in the lamplight with a strange hue, like tarnished silver. In her throat was a small bluish wound; opposite it a gaping hole.

"Shot!" exclaimed Carroll. "Who did it?"

"Some high-minded Caracunan patriot, I suppose."

"Why?"

"Well, I suspect that it was a mistake. From a distance and inside a window, she might easily have been taken for some one else."

Carroll's mind reverted to his companion's ready revolver.

"Yourself, for instance?" he suggested.

"Why, yes."

"Who was she?"

There was left in the Southerner's manner no trace of the cross-examiner. Suspicion had departed from him at the first sight of that old and still face, leaving only sympathy and pity.

"My patient."

"Have you been running a private hospital up here?"

"Oh, no. I took her because there was no other place fit for her to go to. And I had to keep her presence secret, because there's a law against harboring lepers here. A pretty cruel brute of a law it is, too."

"Leprosy!" exclaimed Carroll, looking at that strange silvery face with a shudder. "Isn't it fearfully contagious?"

"Not in any ordinary sense. I was trying a new serum on her, and had planned to smuggle her across to Curacao, when this ended it."

"Curacao? Then that pass for yourself and wife - By the way, that and your coat are over in the thicket, where I dropped them."

"Thank you. But it doesn't say 'wife.' It says simply 'a woman.'"

"And you were encumbering yourself with an unknown leper, at a time like this, just as an act of human kindness?" There was something almost reverential in Carroll's voice.

"Scientific interest, in part. Besides, she wasn't wholly unknown. She's a sort of cousin of Raimonda's."

Carroll's mind flew back to his fatally misinterpreted conversation with the young Caracunan.

"What did he mean by letting me think that you shouldn't associate with Miss Polly?"

"Oh, he had the usual erroneous dread of leprosy contagion, I suppose."

"May I ask you another question, Mr. Per - I beg your pardon, Dr. Pruyn?" said the visitor, almost timidly.

"Perkins will do." The other smiled wanly. "Ask me anything you want to."

"Why did you run away that day on the tram-car?"

"To avoid trouble, of course."

"You? Why, you go about searching for dangerous and difficult jobs. That won't do!"

"Not at all. It's only when I can't get away from them. But I couldn't risk arrest then. Some one would surely have recognized me as Luther Pruyn. You see, I've been here before."

"Then I don't see why they didn't identify you, anyway."

"Three years ago I was much heavier, and wore a full beard. Then these glasses, besides being invaluable for protection, are a pretty thorough disguise."

"So they are. But the game is up now."

"Yes." The scientist drew the sheet back over the dead woman. "I suppose the sharp-shooters who did the job will report me safely out of the way. It's only a question of when the burial party will come for me."

"Then, why are we waiting?" cried Carroll.

"I couldn't leave her lying here," replied the other simply.

The sound of rhythmical labor came back to Carroll's memory.

"You were digging her grave?"

The other nodded. Carroll, stiffly, for his knifed arm was painful, got out of his coat.

"Where's an extra spade?" he asked.

When their labor was over, and the leper laid beneath the leveled soil, Carroll cut two branches from a near-by tree, trimmed them, bound them in the form of a cross, and fixed the symbol firmly in the earth at the dead woman's head.

"That was well thought of," said the scientist. "I'm afraid that wouldn't have occurred to me."

"You can get word to Senor Raimonda?" asked Carroll.

His host nodded. A long silence followed. Carroll broke it: -

"Then there is no further secrecy about this?"

"About what?"

"Her identity." He pointed to the grave.

"No; I suppose not. Why?"

"Because Miss Brewster has a right to know."

"Do you propose to tell her?"

"Yes."

"Very well," agreed the scientist, after a pause for consideration. "But not until after the yacht is at sea."

Carroll did not reply directly to this.

"What shall you do?"

"Get out, if I can. I'm ordered to Curacao. Wisner left word for me."

"Come down the mountain with me."

"Impossible. There are matters here to be attended to."

"Then when will you come down?"

"Before you sail. I must be sure that you get off."

"You'll come to the yacht, then?"

"No."

"I think you should. There are reasons why - why - Miss Brewster -"

"It isn't a question that I can argue," the other cut him off. "I can't do it." There was so much pain in his voice that Carroll forbore to press him. "But I'll ask you to take a note."

Carroll nodded, and his host, disappearing within the quinta, returned almost at once with an envelope on which the address was written in pencil. The Southerner took it and rose from the porch, where he had flung himself to rest.

"Perkins," he said, with some effort, "I've thought and said some hard things about you."

"Naturally enough," murmured the other.

"Do you want me to apologize?"

The scientist stared. "Do you want me to thank you for to-night's work?" he countered.

"No."

"Well -"

"All right."

The two men, different in every quality except that of essential manhood, smiled at each other with a profound mutual understanding. There was a silent handshake, and Carroll set off down the mountain toward the sunrise glow.

XIII

LEFT BEHIND

Dawn crested, poised, and broke in a surf of splendor upon the great mountain-line that overhangs Puerto del Norte. Where, at the corporation dock, there had lurked the shadow of a yacht, gray-black against blue-black, there now swung a fairy ship of purest silver, cradled upon a swaying mirror. Tiny insects, touched to life by the radiance, scuttled busily about her decks and swarmed out upon the dock. The seagoing yacht Polly had awakened early.

Down the mule path that forms the shortest cut from the railway station straggled a group of minute creatures. To one watching from the mountain-side with powerful field-glasses - such as, for example, a convinced and ardent hater of the Caribbean Sea, curled up with his back against a cold and Voiceless rock - it might have appeared that the group was carrying an unusual quantity of hand luggage. Yet they were not porters; so much, even at a great distance, their apparel proclaimed. The pirates of porterdom do not get up to meet five-o'clock-in-the-morning specials in Caracuna.

The little group gathered close at the pier, then separated, two going aboard, and the others disappearing into sundry streets and reappearing presently at the water-front with other figures. The human form cannot be distinctly seen, at a distance of three miles, to rub its eyes; neither can it be heard to curse; but there was that in the newer figures which suggested a sudden and reluctant surrender of sleeping privileges. Had our supposititious watcher possessed an intimate and contemptuous knowledge of Caracuna officialdom, he would have surmised that lavish sums of money had been employed to stir the port and customs officials to such untimely activity.

But not money or any other agency is potent to stir Caracunan officialdom to undue speed. Hence the observer from the heights, supposing that he had a personal interest in the proceedings, might have assured himself of ample time to reach the coast before the formalities could be completed and the ship put forth to sea. Had he presently humped himself to his feet with a sluggish effort, abandoned his field-glasses in favor of a pair of large greenish-brown goggles, and set out on a trail straight down the mountains, staggering a bit at the start, a second supposititious observer of the first supposititious observer - if such cumulative hypothesis be permissible - might have divined that the first supposititious observer was the Unspeakable Perk, going about other people's business when he ought to have been in bed. And so, not to keep any reader in unendurable suspense, it was.

While the Unspeakable Perk was making his way down the dim and narrow trail, another equally weary figure shambled out from the main road upon the flats and made for the landing. The apparel of Mr. Preston Fairfax Fitzhugh Carroll was in a condition that he would have deemed quite unfit for one of his station, had he been in a frame of mind to consider such matters at all. He was not. Affairs vastly more weighty and human occupied his mind. What he most wished was to find Miss Polly Brewster and unburden himself of them.

At the entrance to the pier, he was detained by the American Consul. Cluff came running down the long structure in great strides.

"Moses, Carroll! I'm glad to see you! Where've you been?"

A week earlier, the scion of all the Virginias would have resented this familiarity from a professional athlete. But neither Mr. Carroll's mind nor his heart was a sealed inclosure. He had learned much in the last few days.

"Up on the mountain," he said. "For Heaven's sake, give me a drink, Cluff!"

The other produced a flask.

"You do look shot to pieces," he commented. "Find Perk - Pruyn?"

"Yes. I'll tell you later. Where's Miss Brewster?"

"In her stateroom. Asleep, I guess. Said she wanted rest, and nobody was to disturb her till we sail."

"When do we start?"

"Eight o'clock, they say. That means ten. Will Dr. Pruyn get here?"

"He isn't going with us."

"Oh, no. I forgot his Dutch permit. Well, he'd better use it quick, or he'll go in a box when he does go. I wouldn't insure his life for a two-cent stamp in this country."

"You wouldn't if you'd seen what I saw last night," said the Southerner, very low.

Wisner, the busy, efficient little consul, who had been arranging with the officials for Carroll's embarkation, now returned, bringing with him a viking of a man whom he introduced as Dr. Stark, of the United States Public Health Service.

"Either of you know anything about Dr. Pruyn?" he inquired anxiously.

"He's on his way down the mountain now," said Carroll.

"Good! He's ordered away, I'm glad to say. Just got the message."

"Then perhaps he will go out with us," said Cluff, with obvious relief. "I sure did hate to think of leaving that boy here, with the game laws for goggle-eyed Americans entirely suspended."

"No. He's ordered to Curacao to stay and watch. We've got to get him out to the Dutch ship somehow."

"Couldn't the yacht take him and transfer him outside?" asked Carroll.

"Mr. Carroll," said Dr. Stark earnestly, "before this yacht is many minutes out from the dock, you'll see a yellow flag go up from the end of the corporation pier. After that, if the yacht turns aside or comes back for a package that some one has left, or does anything but hold the straightest course on the compass for the blue and open sea - well, she'll be about the foolishest craft that ever ploughed salt water."

"I suppose so," admitted Carroll. "Well, I have matters to look after on board."

Into Mr. Carroll's cabin it is nobody's business to follow him. A man has a right to some privacy of room and of mind, and if the Southerner's struggle with himself was severe, at least it was of brief duration. Within half an hour, he was knocking at Polly Brewster's door.

"PLEASE go 'way, whoever it is," answered a pathetically weary voice.

"Miss Polly, it's Fitzhugh. I have a note for you."

"Leave it in the saloon."

"It's important that you see it right away."

"From whom is it?" queried the spent voice.

"From Dr. Pruyn."

"I - I don't want to see it."

"You must!" insisted her suitor.

"Did he say I must?"

"No. I say you must. Forgive me, Miss Polly, but I'm going to wait here till you say you'll read it."

"Push it under the door," said the girl resignedly.

He obeyed. Polly took the envelope, summoned up all her spirit, and opened it. It contained one penciled line and the signature: -

Good-bye. All my heart goes with you forever. L. P.

Something fluttered from the envelope to her feet. She stooped and picked it up. It was the tiniest and most delicate of orchids, purple, with a glow of gold at its heart. To her inflamed pride, it seemed the final insult that he should send such a message and such a reminder, without a word of explanation or plea for pardon. Pardon she never would have granted, but at least he might have had the grace of shame.

"Have you read it?" asked the patient voice from without.

"Yes. There is no answer."

"Dr. Pruyn said there wouldn't be."

"Then why are you waiting?"

"To see you."

"Oh, Fitz, I'm too worn out, and I've a splitting headache. Won't it wait?"

"No." The voice was gently inflexible.

"More messages?"

"No; something I must tell you. Will you come out?"

"I suppose so."

Her tone was utterly listless and limp. Utterly listless and limp, she looked, too, as she opened the door and stood waiting.

"Miss Polly, it's about the woman at Perkins's - at Dr. Pruyn's house."

Her eyes dilated with anger.

"I won't hear! How dare you come to me -"

"You must! Don't make it harder for me than it is."

She looked up, startled, and noted the haggard lines in his face.

"I'll hear it if you think I should, Fitz."

"She is dead."

"Dead? His - his wife?"

"She wasn't his wife. She was a helpless leper, whom he was trying to cure with some new serum. He had to do it secretly because there is a law forbidding any one to harbor a leper."

"Oh, Fitz!" she cried. "And she died of it?"

"No. They killed her. Last night."

"They? Who?"

"Government agents, probably. They were after Pruyn."

"How horrible! And - and Mrs. Pruyn. Where was she?"

"There isn't any Mrs. Pruyn. There never was."

"But the Dutch permit! It was for Dr. Pruyn and his wife."

"Sherwen misread the form. So did I. It read for Dr. Pruyn and a woman. He hoped to take her to Curacao and complete his experiment."

"That's what he meant when he spoke of being lawless, and I've been thinking the basest things of him for it!" The girl, dazed by a flash of complete enlightenment, caught at Carroll's arm with beseeching hands. "Where is he, Fitz?"

"On his way down the mountain. Perhaps down here by now."

"He's coming to the ship?" she asked.

"No; he doesn't expect to see you again. He was coming down to make sure that we got off safely."

"Fitz, dear Fitz, I must see him!"

" Miss Polly , " he said miserably , "I'll do anything

I can."

"Oh, poor Fitz!" she cried pityingly, her eyes filling with tears. "I wish for your sake it wasn't so. And you have been so splendid about it!"

"I've tried to make amends, and play fair. It hasn't been easy. Shall I go back and look for him? It's a small town, and I can find him."

"Yes. I'll write a note. No; I won't. Never mind. I'll manage it. Fitz, go and rest. You're worn out," she said gently.

Back into her stateroom went Miss Polly. From that time forth no man saw her nor woman, either, except perhaps her maid, and maids are dark and discreet persons on occasion. If this particular one kept her own counsel when she saw a trim but tremulous figure drop lightly over the starboard rail of the Polly far forward, pick up a small traveling-bag from the pier, step behind the opportune screen of a load of coffee on a flat car, and reappear to view only as a momentary swish of skirt far away at the shore end; if this same maid told Mr. Thatcher Brewster, half an hour later, that Miss Polly was asleep in her stateroom, and begged that she be disturbed on no account, as she was utterly worn out, who shall blame her for her silence on the one occasion or her speech on the other? She was but obeying, albeit with tearful misgivings, duly constituted authority.

Eight o'clock struck on the bell of the little Protestant mission church on the tiny plaza; struck and was welcomed by the echoes, and passed along to eventual silence. Within two minutes after, there was a special stir and movement on the pier, a corresponding stir and movement on board the trim craft, a swishing of great ropes, and a tooting of whistles. White foam churned astern of her. A comic-supplement-looking pelican on a buoy off to port flapped her a fantastic farewell. The blockade-defying yacht Polly was off for blue waters and the freedom of the seas.

On the shore, feeling woefully helpless and alone, she who had been the jewel and joy of the Polly bit her lips and closed her eyes, in a tremulous struggle against the dismal fear: -

"Suppose he doesn't love me, after all!"

XIV

THE YELLOW FLAG

The departing whistle of the yacht Polly struck sharply to the heart of a desolate figure seated on a bench in the blazing, dusty, public square of Puerto del Norte, waiting out his first day of pain. A kiskadee bird, the only other creature foolish enough to risk the hot bleakness of the plaza at that hour, flitted into a dust-coated palm, inspected him, put a tentative query or two, decided that he was of no possible interest, and left the Unspeakable Perk to his own cogitations.

So deep in wretchedness were the cogitations that he did not hear the light, hesitant footstep. But he felt in every vein and fiber the appealing touch on his shoulder.

"Good God! What are YOU doing here?" he cried, leaping to his feet. There was no awkwardness or shyness in his speech now; only wonder-stricken joy.

"I came back to see you."

"But the yacht! Your ship!"

"She has left."

"No! She mustn't! Not without you! You can't stay here. It's too dangerous."

"I must. They think I'm aboard. I left a note for papa. He won't get it until they're at sea. And they can't come back for me, can they?"

"No - yes - they must! I must see Stark and Wisner at once."

"To send me away?"

"Yes."

"Without forgiving me?"

"Forgiving? There's no question of that between you and me."

"There is. Fitzhugh told me everything - all about the poor dead woman."

"Ah, he shouldn't have done that."

"He should!" She stamped a little willful foot. "What else could he do?"

"Why, yes," he agreed thoughtfully. "I suppose that's so. After all, a man can't bear the names that Carroll does and go wrong on the big inner things. He has met his test, and stood it. For he cares very deeply for you."

"Poor Fitz!" she sighed.

"But here we're wasting time!" he cried in a panic. "Where can I leave you?"

"Do you want to leave me?"

"Want to!" he groaned. "Can't you understand that I've got to get you to the yacht!"

"Oh, beetle man, beetle man, don't you WANT me?" she cried dolorously. "Didn't you mean your note?"

"Mean it? I meant it as I've never meant anything in the world. But you - what do you mean? Do you mean that you'll - you'll let the yacht go without you - and - and - and stay here, and m-m-marry me?"

"If you should ask me," she said, half-laughing, half-crying, "what else could I do? I'm alone and deserted. And there's only you in the world."

"Miss P-P-Polly," he began, "I - I can't believe -"

"It's true!" she cried, and held out two yearning hands to him. "And if you stammer and stutter and - and - and act like the Unspeakable Perk NOW, I'll - I'll howl!"

If she had any such project, the chance was lost on the instant of the warning, as he caught her to him and held her close.

"Oh!" she cried, trying to push him away. "Do you know, sir, that this is a public square?"

"Well, I didn't choose it," he reminded her, laughing in pure joy, with a boyish note new to her ear. "Anyway, there are only us two under the sun." And he drew her close again, whispering in her ear.

"Oh - oh, is that the language of medical science?" she reproved.

At this point, generic curiosity overcame the feathered eavesdropper in the tree above.

"Qu'est-ce qu'il dit?" - "What's he say?"

The girl turned a flushed and adorable face upward.

"I won't tell you. It's for me alone," she declared joyously. "But you'll never stop saying it, will you, dear?"

"Never, as long as we both shall live. And that reminds me," he said soberly. "We must arrange about being married."

"Oh, that reminds you, does it?" she mocked. "Just incidentally, like that."

Boom! Boom! Boom! The mission clock kept patiently at it until its suggestion struck in.

"Of course!" he cried. "Mr. Lake, the missionary, will marry us. And we'll have Stark and Wisner for witnesses. How long does it take a bride to get ready? Would half an hour be enough?"

"It's rather a short engagement," she remarked demurely. "But if it's all the time we've got -"

"It is. But, darling, we'll have to ride for it afterward, and get across to the mainland. I've no right to let you in for such a risk," he cried remorsefully.

"You couldn't help yourself," she teased saucily. "I ran you down like one of your own beetles. Besides, what does that permit for the Dutch ship say?"

"That's for myself and a woman - the leper woman. Not for myself and my wife."

"Well, I'm a woman, aren't I? And it doesn't say that the woman MUSTN'T be your wife." She blushed distractingly.

"Caesar! Of course it doesn't! What luck! We'll be in Curacao to-morrow. I must see Wisner about getting us off. But, Polly, dearest one, you're sure? You haven't let yourself be carried away by that foolishness of mine yesterday?"

"Sure? Oh, beetle man!" She put her hands on his shoulders and bent to his ear.

The sulphur-colored winged Paul Pry stuck an impertinent head out from behind a palm leaf.

"Qu'est-ce qu'elle dit? Qu'est-ce qu'elle dit?"

For the second and last time in his adult life the beetle man threw a stone at a bird.

Four hours later six powerful black oarsmen rowed a boat containing two passengers and practically no luggage out across the huge lazy swells of the Caribbean toward a smudge of black smoke.

"Look!" cried that one of the passengers who wore huge goggles. "There goes the flag!"

A square of yellow bunting slid slowly up the pierhead staff of the dock corporation, and spread in the light shore breeze.

"That's the modern flaming sword," he continued. "The color stirs something inside me. Ugly, isn't it?"

"It is ugly," she confessed thoughtfully. "Yet it's the flag we fight under, too, isn't it? And we'd fight for it if we had to, just as we fought for the other - our own."

"I love your 'we,'" he laughed happily.

She nestled closer to him.

"Are you still hating the Caribbean?"

"I? I'm loving it the second-best thing in the world."

"But I loved it first," she reminded him jealously. "Dearest," she added, with one of her swift swoops of thought, "what was that funny title the British Secretary of Legation had?"

"What? Oh, Captain the Honorable Carey Knowles?"

"Yes. Well, I shall have a much nicer, more picture-sque title than that when we come back to Caracuna - dear, dirty, dangerous, queer, riotous, plague-stricken old Caracuna!"

"Then my liege ladylove intends to come back?" he asked.

"Of course. Some time. And in Caracuna I shall insist on being Mrs. the Unspeakable Perk."

www.ingramcontent.com/pod-product-compliance
Lightning Source LLC
Chambersburg PA
CBHW050031180626
46810CB00002B/665